Bitter Circumstances

Dawn Elizabeth Clower

PublishAmerica
Baltimore

First printing

ISBN: 1-59129-840-7
PUBLISHED BY PUBLISHAMERICA BOOK PUBLISHERS
www.publishamerica.com
Baltimore

Printed in the United States of America

To my husband,
Heath,
my greatest support has been from you and I love you
more than I can express in words.

This book is dedicated to Wendy White.
Thank you for believing in me all these years.

Prologue

His eyes scanned the schoolyard for a glimpse of her face. It wasn't hard to spot her and that started thoughts reeling in his head. What he wanted and what he could have seemed like one in the same. He would get his wish. It may be the only way to make her realize how much love he really had in his heart for her. Her purity was such a scarcity in this world, but he knew she would be glad when it was over. He wondered to himself if one time would be nearly enough or if there would be more encounters. He wondered if the relationship would be as good (probably better) as the one she was in currently. Never mind that. That just seemed to burst his bubble. Thoughts returned to evil, and he mentally schemed even more.

He sat behind the steering wheel in the beat up old '82 Buick watching as she came out of the gymnasium. Her hair was blowing in the wind and she looked just like a princess. His heart nearly rose from his chest at the sight of her. He came unglued at the thought that she would be getting into a car with his nemesis.

He knew he could change her life forever but she didn't seem interested in anything but that boyfriend of hers. With a scathing and vindictive tongue, he groused to himself, "You know you can have anyone you want and you chose that other guy. You think he's so much better than anyone because he's just like you. I'll show you, you little tease. You'll see, baby. It's not gonna be long now." His gold colored eyes crossed maniacally as he pressed his fingers up against the window. She passed by and crawled into the little sports car with the enemy.

Chapter 1

As the phone began to ring, Barbara slammed her knife onto the kitchen counter, obviously put out at the thought of being interrupted. She picked up the receiver to hear, "Mark? NO!" She mordantly made her way down the hall to a room closed behind a door donning all sorts of skateboard paraphernalia and symbols she was sure belonged to Satan himself.

The room was pounding with loud music so she attempted an even louder bang on the door. "Mark, turn that mess down! The phone is for you. I'm going to hang up on whoever it is in two seconds." She meandered back to the kitchen alone with her head bobbing up and down telling Mark all about it. It would have made an excellent speech on all the ways to annoy your grandmother, had he been present to listen. Under her not-so-quiet breath, she pouted and remarked, "What do you think you are calling here, thinking that my voice would be Mark? I am a woman and I deserve some respect." Members of the family would have disagreed with that point.

Inside the blue room lit with a black light, the scenery complemented the door. Mark, a normal sixteen-year-old boy, sat posed at his desk in front of a computer, talking into a microphone and looking at the screen while typing in computer lingo, setting up some sort of a program. "I hate that old woman. She drives me nuts."

A southern teenage boy voice hitting the onset of puberty squeaked out of the speaker of the computer, "Man, what's going on tonight? Can you drive your car?"

"Why do we have to use my car? You've got transportation."

"Man, my car busted on the way home from work last night. It'll probably cost me a couple hundred to fix. 'Bout you come over here? My step-dad'll be gone. Tonight he's drinking cuz he and Mom got in a fight over somethin' stupid. All I could hear was yellin' this mornin. I swear I'll kill him someday. I will. My mom ain't strong enough to leave him, so maybe I ought to force her."

"Buck, James isn't anything to be scared of. He's just a skinny drunk. You could take him easy. I'll be over there in a little while. All right. See ya." He hung up with a poke of a finger on the keyboard. How convenient to have the computer as your sole source of communication. He turned off the computer and without so much as a good-bye or glance to his grandmother, ran out the door, with car keys in his hand.

As Mark streaked by the kitchen, Barbara and Abby were working hard on a meal that may or may not be eaten by a whole family. Abby had her hair up in a ponytail and wore a T-shirt with a pair of blue jeans. She was beautiful and at the age of forty-three, no one would say she looked a day over thirty-five. Barbara piped her two cents, which was really worth nothing.

"You are just too lenient on your boy. You know he is up to no good but you don't change any of the habits he has. Those friends of his are the worst I've seen. I think he's into bad things and I wouldn't be surprised if he were going off to practice some sort of Satanic ritual. He's got those kind of eyes you know. My son, Glenn, bless his heart, was such a well-mannered boy growing up and he did so well for himself, and for you. It's a shame that you've allowed your son to become such a rebel."

"Barbara." Abby knew not to press the issue or the conversation would never end but she was tempted and fate played its hand. "As you know, Mark makes excellent grades, is a great computer genius, and I don't think anyone in the world would argue the love he has for his sister. I think he's a great boy, just wanting to be himself and I can't fault him for that."

Interrupting, "Well, I frankly don't care what you can't fault him for. If you ask me, he needs a good spanking. Tell me that boys will be boys. You just don't do it right. Now let me try and he'll be doing everything I say and adding M'ams and Sirs to it. None of that back talking, running out the house or acting like he's the only one who exists." She stifled a grin but softly giggled. "You are just way too spineless. Now darlin', hand me that oregano."

Abby attempted to change the subject to something that would not cause Barbara to go into one of her rantings, but this was apparently not it. "Glen should be home soon. He called earlier and said that his client was running over to bring him some papers for the arraignment tomorrow. I'll be glad when this guy gets out of the way and I can have my husband back."

"Darling, quit your griping. It's pathetic. What I suggest is that you be thankful that my son is smart enough and successful enough to pay for all the nice things you have. If it weren't for his job and the partnership in his law firm, you would have a lot more to gripe about. I never saw anyone so ungrateful and selfish as you in all my life. You should be ashamed for talking about him that way. He does everything in the world for you and those self-centered grandchildren of mine. How one person can gripe so much is beyond me. Pass me the flour and the chicken." Barbara pushed Abby out of the way and replied condescendingly, "Why don't you let me finish this? Go set the table would you?"

Obediently, Abby walked out with dishes and silverware in hand and set the table. The doorbell rang and in walked the neighbor, Carla, a sturdy woman about the age of Abby.

She had her hands put behind her back and head hung low. "Hey girl. I was wondering if you were busy." She raised her head slowly and put her hand on Abby's shoulder. "I would like to talk to you in private for a moment." She shot a glance at Barbara who was standing in the doorway hoping to eavesdrop. Offended by the remark, Barbara flitted back into the kitchen and mumbled some more.

Abby joined Carla outside on the front steps. The gigantic columns and the ancient Magnolia trees provided beautiful and cooling shade on the bright hot Spring day. "Carla, you look so upset, are you okay? What's wrong?"

Barbara's nosey image gawked out the window unbeknownst to the two friends. She listened closely but heard nothing. In a wave of her special brilliance, she slowly opened the door to catch a few words of the conversation, but caught nothing as they turned around glaring at her. To cover her own butt, she pouted, "I believe the table isn't set yet, Abby. I guess I will have to do it myself."

Abby didn't try to excuse her to Carla. Carla was Abby's best friend and was always privy to the wonderful over-exaggerations of her mother-in-law. She knew it was best to just ignore Barbara. "I'd say she's in one of her moods, but she's always in one of her moods. You know, you'd think this was her house the way she takes over. Okay, Carla. Go ahead and tell me. What is it?"

Carla began "I don't know if you and Glen are having problems, and this may be none of my business, but if it were me I would want to know."

"What? Just say it."

"I saw Glen in a restaurant with a woman yesterday."

"A client. Right?"

"Abby, she didn't appear to be doing business. I could be making it into something it isn't, but I wanted to let you know. I am your friend and I would *not* tell you something just to hurt you. You know that don't you?"

Shocked and confused at the news, Abby calmly looked at her friend and with a long deep breath, spoke.

"Yeah, I know you wouldn't hurt me on purpose."

Abby stewed over the thoughts going wild in her head and then she finally let it pour out of her. Everything she'd ever feared and felt came out in a flood of words.

"It's been so long since we have been intimate. My gosh, it's been so long since we've even talked or even looked at each other in the face. This past year he hasn't spent more than eight hours a day at the house, six of which are spent sleeping. Everything is always business. He missed Melanie when she made homecoming queen. He has no idea what is going on with Mark. Of course Mark is partly to blame for that, but he doesn't even make time to see *me* when he's here. He comes in, visits with Barbara and eats at his desk while he works on some briefs or something. He goes to bed and then leaves before I even get up. I figured it was business, all this time. I can't let my family fall apart. Barbara would just love to see me wallow in misery over her son. I used to stand up to people. I was never a doormat but look at me! People have been taking advantage of me for the past twenty years."

As the thoughts came to her, she let them out in words. Carla just listened, as any good friend would do. Even though the thoughts were now more of Barbara's role in her marriage problems than Glenn's role.

The blame became easy when put in Barbara's direction. "After Glenn's dad died, we let her move in and she's been the queen of *my* castle, telling me that I am so selfish, never right, a horrible mother, and that my cooking stinks. I'm letting her take over my children, my husband. Oh my gosh! That's the problem. That's why Glenn and I never communicate. How could I have been so dumb?"

"Abby, you're not dumb. You are a good woman. It seems difficult to reason right now, but when you talk to Glenn, I'm sure everything will work itself out. You just got taken advantage of."

"Carla, that's not what I mean. Don't you see? He never left his mother. When we got married he was always going over to her house to see her, he called her every day. He didn't even come see me that much when we were dating. He never let go of her. So much for the Bible verse, 'And a man should leave his mother and father and cleave to his wife.' We are a threesome. And frankly, Carla, I don't want to be married to her. I need him but his mother has to go. The problem is that every time I get around her I weaken and can't stand up for myself."

Carla became confused at the turn of conversation. "Abby, I think we're going off the subject. Glenn may be cheating on you and you're worried more about his mother. So she's overbearing and critical, is that a reason to blame her for your husband's infidelity? Think about what you're doing."

"No! Really, it makes sense. She always made me feel so insufficient and he seemed to believe everything she said. I was always wrong in her eyes and she made sure that he would agree with her. He is to blame for his cheating, but she is solely responsible for dividing my family." She stood up quickly and looked around, sporting a new air of confidence. She opened the front door and looked back at Carla. "I do believe I have a family to repair and a mother-in-law to get rid of. I'll call you later."

She grabbed a pair of keys on the foyer table and ran out to the car, speeding out of the driveway.

Barbara stood at the kitchen window glaring and muttered to herself, "Well, you little snit! You left me to do all the work. That is just like you. No wonder Glenn never comes home."

Melanie was sitting in the front seat of Jason's car. She had long blonde hair pulled back from her face. Her cheeks were rosy from the sun and the freckles on her face were appearing through the translucent ivory of her skin. She had a very shapely figure and carried herself with respect and dignity. There was no image of impurity on her character. Jason was the type of rugged good-looking guy that many people stare at but only few would actually talk to. He was tough, beautiful and muscular, but his heart and soul were as gentle as a kitten. They were a perfect match and the fact that he was in college and she was a senior in high school made her girlfriends completely envious.

Jason was studying to become a youth minister. It was his passion to work with youth. He was constantly focused on how God's Word could be part of everyday life and how he could affect even one kid's life. He was a promoter of the abstinence campaign at the high school and his church youth group. Melanie's devotion was true and she was as much a promoter of abstinence as Jason.

They sat in the car at her house after driving home from her cheerleading practice. Melanie listened to Jason, "some of the guys I know are having a party at the Student Union and I thought we could go tonight. Are you okay with that?"

Melanie's eyes sparkled and Jason noticed how they resembled the same color that shone in the sky. "Okay, yes, but I don't want to stay as long as we did last time. That girl who kept hitting on you in front of me will probably show up and I don't think I can take her company again."

"Yeah, Kari's quite a flirt. But she's harmless."

"Jason, don't you mean HOPELESS? I'm not jealous. There's a difference is being a flirt because you are fun and being a flirt because you're desperate."

"So are you saying you have to be desperate to come on to me?" He grinned and the dimple in his left cheek was enough to make her smile. "Oh come on, Mel. Give her a break. She's lonely. We should encourage her to branch out with other girls and to start building a friendship. She seems to hang out where the guys always are."

"Okay. I'll become her life-long friend if she's at the party tonight," she smirked. "Do you want to come inside and eat supper? I hope everyone will be there for a change. It's starting to get lonely at home. Even when people are there, it seems to be like a museum. No one talks. Everyone just stares at the walls. It wasn't this bad until Grandma moved in last year. I really don't know what her deal is with my mom, but she is so hateful to her. Mom can't do anything right. It's always, 'No, Abby, that's not it, let *me* show you how.' I get so sick of her. Have you heard how she talks to Mark?"

He stumbled for a courteous way to say no, but all he could come out with was "Well, I don't think we should eat here. Not if you're going to be uncomfortable." He covered his tracks well.

Not surprisingly, she understood. Frankly, she was relieved a little. "Please just come in with me to let them know we're going out to eat and to a party."

Barbara immediately faced them and exclaimed, "Melanie, your mother, so she calls herself, is not here. Do you know where she went? She was talking to that screwy neighbor Carla and then just took off in the car. She didn't even finish helping with dinner."

"I have no idea, but she probably had an errand to run. Where's Mark?"

"Probably having something tattooed or pierced."

"Grandma!" she almost lashed out, but bit her tongue and said, "Jason and I are eating out." Melanie turned to the door and pulled Jason's arm to leave. She looked back and without a thought, let her tongue out of the muzzle. "As for Mom and Mark, I'm glad they don't have to be here to listen to you gripe all night. Bye!"

She let the door slam behind her and looked innocently at Jason, "What?" He just opened her car door and helped her in.

Chapter 2

Abby marched hastily past the secretary and barged into Glenn's office unannounced. The desk was piled with paperwork and behind the desk seated in the large leather-rolling chair was a young and dignified lady in a blue suit with her hair swept up. Her head was relaxed as his hands massaged her neck. The office door slammed shut and Glenn sprung to the other side of the desk when he noticed Abby in his office.

Abby addressed the lady, "Do you mind leaving while I talk to my husband?" The lady scurried out the door but in the heat of the moment, she left her purse on the chair.

Glenn was a handsome man who looked the part of the lawyer that he was. He was a high-powered, high-dollar lawyer and he loved the title as well as the prestige. When he and Abby married, they were both in college. He had every intention of being the best and the most wealthy. He wanted to be impressive, not only to her but everyone else. He chose Abby for her looks, in the beginning, but her sweet, honest, and loyal demeanor made him fall head over heels in a hurry. They married and he achieved everything he set out to.

He looked right at Abby and said, "Honey, I know what you want. I'm not going to pretend that I can't read that look on your face. We have a lot to talk about."

Abby laughed loudly, "I should say we do. But, before you start explaining, I want to say, I feel like I'm partially to blame for this."

"How did you find out? It doesn't matter, but I just want to know?"

"You're right. It doesn't matter. I'm not telling you. The fact is that I am so hurt and so angry at you right now for what you've done. For what you're doing. But, I'm not blaming you for everything. I should have seen this. I shouldn't have been so blind. Glenn, as much as I want to hate you now, I still love you that much more."

His face was bowing to the ground in shame and yet her words at that moment picked up his eyes and he glanced up.

She continued, "I feel like a fool. I feel like years have gone by and we have let Satan pull us into this pit. We aren't going to survive without some work on both our parts. Do you want us to work? Just answer me this, do you want to be with me?"

Just then the door opened and the lady waltzed in with less dignity than before and slid up to the desk to lift her purse off the paperwork pile. Then, with no eye contact, she explained the obvious. "I forgot my purse."

Without patience in her voice, Abby curtly exclaimed, "Well, now you've got it. What are you waiting for? Leave!"

Glenn spoke up and reached for the lady's arm, "Come over here." He pulled her to his desk. His eyes looked sad as he said, "Abby, there is nothing else to say. I want you to leave and we'll talk when I get home.

The lady shook, "Glenn, what are you doing? Don't do that to me."

"Shut up! Abby, leave!"

Abby bowed out the door and quietly stated, "Very well. Good-bye Glenn."

Shocked, the lady pulled her arm out of Glenn's hand and yelled, "How dare you put me in that kind of position. I have no idea what is going on with you and your wife. My husband will not be happy with this. You're fired!" She ran toward the door and looked back at him with fire in her eyes. She slammed the door, and Glenn could still hear her high heels clicking on the marble floors until she got on the elevator.

In one frustrated gesture Glenn scraped his hands down his desk pushing everything onto the floor. The receptionist heard the commotion but with all of the entering and exiting, she thought it best to stay out at her post. Glenn rose to the large wall of windows and peered out, watching his Abby get into her luxury car and drive away. Tears streamed down his face as he fell to his knees and wondered what he was doing.

The music was loud and obnoxious. The room pulsated to the beat while the people danced. It was almost impossible to make out who people were, but even if you knew to whom you were speaking to, the noise would blare out any chance of decent conversation.

Melanie looked comfortable but beautiful dressed in a cool crisp white short-sleeved shirt and denim capris. Jason wore a t-shirt and jeans. The couple seemed to everyone else like the perfect couple and most girls knew Jason was hands off. Guys who were interested in the idea of seeking out Melanie were mostly into just that, the idea. It was a disappointment to both sexes all the way around.

Melanie was still in high school but Jason loved her. He was persuaded early in their relationship that this was "the one." She took a little more persuading but the relationship grew to a long two year standing and when he went to college nothing changed. The plans remained the same. After he graduated, they would get married. Both had been saving themselves for the one God sent to them. It was so important to them, that they remained faithful in their belief even through the difficult puberty and coming of age years.

Melanie never felt very content in the party scene. She was more of a quiet girl, but she never underestimated the power of a little fun. She had a crazy streak that Jason was in love with. The adventurous beauty could get Jason to go rock climbing, white river rafting, and even to a few chick flicks. The party was just like every other one that Jason's fraternity had, but the uneasy feeling there this specific night was more than she could take. She suddenly turned around with a feeling of being watched. "Who's that guy over there?" As she asked, the guy turned and ducked toward the dance floor.

Jason looked but didn't catch a glimpse. "I don't know which one you mean."

Without seeing the face closely, she couldn't identify him on the dance floor either. "Shoot, he's gone."

"What's wrong? Do you think you know him?"

"I don't, I don't think so. He was staring at me. He's been staring at me since we got here. Oh well, it's probably nothing." She shook it off and sipped her Coke.

"Yeah, it's probably just that he can't take his eyes off you. I can't." The remark slipped by her completely. She couldn't wait to leave the party. She felt out of place with his college friends and neither of them was very crazy about the atmosphere.

Chapter 3

Abby looked pale and her eyes bloodshot as she walked to the kitchen in her robe. She saw Mark getting some milk out of the fridge. Glad to see a part of her family, she walked over to him and touched his shoulder. He noticed her appearance and it worried him though he couldn't seem too interested. It could ruin his plans for the evening.

"Honey, are you leaving tonight? I mean, I just wondered if you would want to stay around and keep me company or if this was just a pit stop?" Her eyes searched his for some sense of comfort and she thought she saw a glimpse, until he came back with the remark, "Buck's out in the car. We just stopped to get some CD's and stuff. I gotta go. I'll be back later."

She struggled to hold back tears and fought for words to make him stay. All she came up with was, "Mark, I need to, I need to. Umm, I just wanted to let you know I love you." She hugged him and then quickly pulled away frightfully aware that she had invaded the teenage space.

He felt her urgency and knew he should be more sympathetic to her. But heck, Buck was in the car. "Yeah Mom. See ya." He sauntered out the back door and then managed to inch out a quiet, "I love you, Mom."

Inside the car, the bass pumped loudly but the twin pipes on the large, loaded, royal blue pickup drowned the words out.

"Mark, what in the world took so long? Your grandma corner ya?" Buck joked.

Mark snickered and then said, "My mom's acting weird. I hope she's okay."

"Why, what happened?"

"Not sure. She said she loved me. I think she'd been crying." He let go of the emotion and quickly slipped back into 'cool boy' mode. "Oh well. She'll be fine." Deep down he was still wondering.

A magnificent grandfather clock stood prominent in the foyer and it struck a beautiful tune announcing the time was 11:00 p.m. Abby sat wrapped in an afghan with her Bible open. She had fallen asleep and the clock woke her a little, but not as much as the shutting of the front door. She knew it was Glenn. He laid his briefcase on the foyer table and made his way to the study. The arched doorway showcased his figure, which usually stood stately and demanding. It now looked ashamed and sedate. He paused before he approached her. With caution, he sat on the chair next to hers and she glanced down at her Bible. She couldn't make out words through the tears. They poured out and she couldn't stop them from falling.

He quietly said, "Abby, I'm sorry for what happened today. I think you need to know who that was." She didn't want to know but her voice wouldn't produce sound and she couldn't stop him.

"I'm not having an affair. That was my client's wife who was bringing over some papers. Her husband is going to prison for fraud. She was upset. I was consoling her. She was signing over the papers verifying she had no knowledge of the transactions. That's the truth Abby, I swear. I guess I should feel flattered that you were jealous."

Abby worked up her courage and asked, "Do you love me?"

"I do love you. Not only do I love you but I have built my world around trying to please you and the kids. I feel I never do."

"That's not true. You have pleased me by being my husband. I think our problem is that we haven't spent any time getting to know each other lately. We've lost touch and I feel that part of it is due to the fact that your mother lives here. Actually, I feel that your mother has lived with us since we got married."

He turned defensive. "What the heck does that mean? You never liked my mom. She may be rough around the edges, but she is a good woman."

"Do you realize that she still rules your life? You're like a little child who still lives with his mom. She tells you to jump and you do. She dislikes something and you don't do it. The worst part of the whole thing is that I conform to what she wants instead of standing up for you. I want to be your ally. I never build you up when she's tearing you down. I just agree with her so I don't get on her bad side, well, any more than I already am."

Glenn retorted defensively, "Don't blame our problems on my mom. If it weren't for her, this house would be a wreck. We would never eat. It's a good thing that she is here. She at least cares that I have spent a day at the office, working for a living."

"Are you saying that I can't keep a house? What about the meals I cooked? Oh, but they're not Mama's meals. And I sure don't clean the toilet like Mama. NOOOO!!! You're so transparent. I can't believe I didn't see it before now." Her hands rested on her hips.

"Abby, you are yelling. You'll wake her up."

"It's my house too, Glenn. If she wakes up, great! Maybe she'll catch my hint and LEAVE! I detest that you can't see how your mom has you under her little finger and how much she tries to dismiss me from your life. She would love for me to be gone and you be her little baby again."

"What do you want me to do? Dad's gone and she has no place to go."

Abby sat down on the chair arm looking exhausted and let down. "Since she moved in, my life has revolved around satisfying her. I want to satisfy you and be your wife again. Glen, you and I don't even look at each other in the eye anymore. Can you honestly say that you even find me remotely attractive?"

There was a strong hush in the room as she waited what seemed like an eternity. Did she ask the wrong question? Was it the wrong time? She prayed for an honest answer, but not this one.

He looked torn as he could only utter, "Abby, I'm going to sleep on the couch tonight and we can mull over what has been said. We need to talk about this tomorrow, honey. It's been a long day and I'm just exhausted."

He turned to leave the study but her quiet voice caught him. It was the same voice he fell in love with years before. He'd forgotten all about what he loved in her until now.

"Glenn, I love you. Please don't shut me out. You can't keep rescheduling our relationship. This isn't a courtroom where you can just reconvene at a later time. This is a marriage and I need you to be here. You need me to be here and our children need us here." Tears streamed down her face and he knew he couldn't look for fear he would crumble. He was a tough man and an even tougher lawyer but nothing was more laborious on him than hurting his own wife. He slowly stepped out into the hallway out of Abby's sight and tears began to flow as he made his way into the bedroom and shut the door.

Abby fell back into the chair and clutched her Bible closely to her breast. She was humiliated by her husband but still strong enough to admit to God how weak she felt. "God, my marriage is in your hands. Please help us, please Lord, don't let my marriage end."

Glenn opened the bedroom door with every intention of going back in to talk to Abby, however, he was stopped by the appearance of his mother making a trek to the study. He stood outside in the hall listening for what could be a bomb exploding.

Barbara's voice, loud, obnoxious and completely disregarding of the hour of the evening complained. "Abby, would you shut up? I can't get any sleep with you rattling on in here."

This was Abby's home and the time had finally arrived when she let the sparks fly. Without rising out of the chair, she simply looked up with staid eyes and said "Barbara! I want you out of my house. You might want to start packing up. You will be leaving soon!"

Barbara stood dismayed and Abby just looked back down and opened her Bible. Glenn was overcome with pride at Abby's boldness and for the first time able to see exactly what his mother was about. In the midst of the pride, he was uncertain if he liked what he had just seen.

The party ended and both Melanie and Jason were equally grateful. It was about one in the morning. The rules in the Student Union were that all students had to leave at one o'clock a.m. Melanie was tired and she couldn't help keep herself from complaining about the immature friends Jason had. He couldn't defend them very well, because in actuality they were extremely juvenile.

"I can't believe you like those people, Jason!"

Having heard about enough of that kind of talk, he finally remarked, "Melanie, if you would come off your pedestal once in a while, you might get to know some pretty neat people. *All* of my friends are not that bad. You just refuse to have a good time unless we are around your little high school friends. I'm not complaining about all of them, but you know good and well that a few of your friends are way too immature. I fear for our future government if they are what are out there."

"Oh, well isn't that the pot calling the kettle black! You and your little buddies can't go one day without acting like morons. I saw how you all acted tonight. Funny thing about it, Jason, you aren't like that and I know it. You are a lot better than those guys and I would think that you would have picked a better group to hang around. The only one who didn't act ridiculous was the one who kept staring at me all night and he left early."

In anger, Jason lashed out, "If you don't like it, maybe I need to upgrade to a girl my own age. One who is on my own level?"

"That's fine with me. Stop the car."

"Don't be a baby! I am at least driving you home."

"Stop the car!"

He kept driving and yelled back, "Don't be crazy."

"I said stop the car!"

Without thinking logically, he slammed on the brakes and Melanie jumped out of the car, slamming the door as he skidded off leaving tracks. She began to think about what she'd done. It was dark, late and she had no money or her cell phone to call her parents or a friend. She began to cry and walk.

Suddenly she heard a screech round the corner and, assuming it was Jason, turned around to see him. It wasn't Jason's car, but a dark colored older model Buick had ridden up onto the curb. The car pulled off the curb and started to drive toward her slowly. Afraid, she turned and began to walk but noticed that the car kept following her. Her heart pounded and her feet began to feel like lead, as the car sped up and shined bright lights on her. She crossed the street and the car still followed her and then quickly pulled in front of her, cutting her off. She turned to run and a man jumped from the car and chased her. With a thunderous blow to her head, he slammed her down on the ground and covered her face with his jacket. He had her hands pinned under his knees and she was so weak from her head injury, she couldn't fight back. "You get what you deserve, you phony! All of you girls are fakes." He was messing around with something, though she didn't know what. He finally took the jacket from her face to reveal a horrifying clown face-mask and then a mechanical noise emerged. Laughing maniacally, he pulled her shirt in two and began to tie her hands to the tree.

She pleaded, "Oh please don't do this. Please. Please don't hurt me."

He chuckled, "You were looking at me tonight!" Somehow the face mask made his voice sound mechanical. He continued teasing and taunting, "I saw you with your boyfriend. You looked happy then. What happened? Did you fight with Jason? Did Jason give you the boot? Was he not happy with you? Melanie, he's not happy with anyone who looks like a clown when she goes out. You're a phony, a fake."

"How do you know my name? What do you want from me? I promise I won't tell anyone about this if you'll just let me go." Tears streamed down her face, and as if out of love, he wiped them from her cheek and kissed her gently. She attempted to move her face to the side but he grabbed her harshly and forced his lips on hers.

"But, aren't we having fun? You should tell everyone about this. This absolutely will be the most memorable thing you will ever have to tell. But on the other hand, I really don't care if you don't tell anyone. I only know, I will be a part of your history." He laughed and the sound echoed in her ears. "Jason doesn't know what he's got. You should try Vegas with an act like yours. Like I'd let you go now! You tempt me at the party by staring at me and then act like I don't mean anything to you. What's wrong with this picture? I'd like to be able to go back to the dorm and tell Jason what he's missing out on. You see, Melanie, I know that you two are virgins, or should I say *were* virgins? So, you were both waiting till you were married. You'll never see that happen. I don't think you really want to wait anyway." His voice got cold and deep and then her cries disappeared into wails of screams and yelps.

He grabbed her neck and choked her and then proceeded to abuse her far more than any body should be able to withstand. When she finally passed out, about three hours later, he looked at her in utter disgust, got up, walked away, returned to his car and drove away, as if nothing happened at all.

The sun came up and the park began to bustle with joggers and dog walkers before the work hours began. Melanie gradually came to and the sun shown down in her eyes while she could see the sky turning from a dark gray to a deep cornflower blue. Her head throbbed as she tried to make out the figure in front of her. It was the clown face she had fallen asleep to before. She let out a blood-curdling scream and turned away from the image as a man came running through the bushes and grabbed her. He startled her so badly that she immediately recalled the events of the evening and was sure it was him.

The man in the blue jogging suit slowly untied her hands from the tree trunk and calmly said, "Ok, don't worry, I'm gonna get you some help. Honey, it'll be ok." He looked around at the audience that had gathered and frustrated at the complacency said, "Can someone please call 911!"

He took his shirt off and carefully put it over her bare body in an attempt to allow her some modesty and to keep her warm. She was shaking and crying as he held her. Onlookers stood in shock as one lady dialed the emergency number and frantically exclaimed, "Yes. I'm at Benchfield Park near the fountains. There's a girl here. I think she's been attacked. We need an ambulance fast."

Melanie moaned and pleaded to her gentle rescuer, "Please help me. Please don't let him get me." He reassured her over and over until the police showed up at the scene.

Chapter 4

Glenn was still asleep on the couch when the dissonant ring came over the room. He sat up startled and looked at his watch. It was only ten till six. Who could be calling this early? He grappled wearily for the phone on the end table. His groggy voice chortled out a weak "Hello." Within a second, he sat up completely alert and processed the information. With a slam of the phone on the table, he screamed, "Abby, get down here. It's Melanie."

She rounded the corner in her robe and house shoes. "She was on the phone?"

"She's in the hospital!" he retorted. They scrambled for their clothes quickly and ran to Mark's room. They entered without noticing the sign that impolitely asked that all adults stay out. He sat up in the bed and quietly said, "What's wrong?"

"Your father said that Melanie is in the hospital. We need to go, now!"

"Get some clothes on. We'll be in the car. Please make it quick, son." Glenn commanded.

Mark stood up from the sheets and threw on a shirt and grabbed the pants from last night and was out the door as soon as he slid into his flip-flops. He heard his mom asking questions and realized that no one knew anything. "Glenn, what happened? Was she in a wreck?"

He teared up as he held his wife's hand and said, "I don't know."

Barbara wandered out into the hallway with the brilliant idea that she should go as well. "Glenn, get in the car and I'll drive you down to the hospital. Mark and Abby can come later when Melanie is up to having visitors."

With it being the worst time for her shenanigans, Abby struck out, "We are hardly visitors, Barbara." Glenn interrupted as he and Abby looked at each other. He protested to his mother, making Abby take notice as he calmly said, "Mom, you will stay here. Abby and Mark and I will go to the hospital. I think she just needs her family right now. Can you call Abby's mom and dad and let them know? We'll call you when we get to see her."

Barbara's eyes widened at the thought that she was being made to wait. "Glenn, that's the most ridiculous thing I've ever heard. Melanie needs me!"

"No, she needs her mom and dad. Don't argue with me on this, Mother. Just make sure you call Ben and Sandra. The number is by the phone in the kitchen." Not attempting to look at the anger in Barbara's face, knowing it would only cause more exhausting arguments; they all got in the car and drove away.

As they arrived at the hospital, the three ran in and Glenn demanded to know any information. The nurses' station bustled with workers and even more patients' families requesting information about patients, bills and bathrooms. A tidy looking nurse stood at a computer terminal and looked straight at the panic of Glenn Crawford and quietly asked, "Sir, may I be of assistance to you?"

Without hesitation, Glenn spoke patiently and assertively, "My daughter, Melanie Crawford, where is she? Can you let me see her?"

"Oh yes, sir. The doctor would like to talk to you about your daughter's injuries. He is in a consultation with another patient if you would be so kind as to wait in the waiting room."

He didn't like that answer and refused her kind retort with a bit of his own. "No. You tell me where she is. He can talk to me in there. I want to see my daughter. NOW!" A shy yet forceful smile crossed his lips.

Obviously this wasn't the first type of situation like this, no other nurses looked up or even gave thought to what was happening at the nurses' station. She firmly answered, "Sir, I understand you are upset but Dr. Keller has asked that no one be permitted to see her until he talks to them. A rape case is a very serious trauma..."

"What? NO!" Glenn and Abby both interrupted with shock at the news that it was rape that brought their daughter to this hospital. Abby grabbed Glenn's arm and moved him over to put herself in front of the nurse. "It can't be rape. What, w-w-w-when, wh-who? Jason?" Words barely made their way out of her mouth and the nurse was poorly aware that nobody had been informed of the cause of injuries.

She tried to continue with her sad little speech that she apparently gave to all patient's families, "…it is important that you understand what your daughter has been through and how she looks right now. She has very serious injuries."

An older man in a white coat, looking very distinguished and very busy, walked up behind Glenn and the nurse gave the doctor a nod to signal it was his turn to take over. The relief couldn't have come at a better time as the nurse pulled away and went to pour a cup of stale, strong black coffee.

"Mr. and Mrs. Crawford, I presume?"

"I'm praying that you are the doctor who can tell me about my daughter. What is wrong? Can't we see her?"

"Mr. and Mrs. Crawford, I want to explain what happened to Melanie. She will be moved to ICU when she's stable and a bed becomes available, under very close observation. She sustained several blows to the chest, abdomen and head. Her heart rate is stable but we feel it necessary to watch her overnight for any internal bleeding or swelling of the head. She has a concussion on the back of her head. We know you haven't heard any of the details, the concussion most likely happened shortly after the actual rape. She was found tied to a tree and then beaten in between several times of being molested. We feel that she was probably unconscious at that time. Now, she probably won't remember much, but the memory will sooner or later allow her to know what happened. That in itself will be very painful. The memory can either help us or hinder us. The police may be able to help catch whoever did this, *if* she remembers anything and wants to tell us. Do you have any questions? If not we can go see her."

Without a bit of hesitation, Glenn and Abby sounded, "Yes, we want to see her." The doctor led the Crawfords down the pristine and bustling hallway to a room with several beds, machines, pumps, and monitors. Nurses checked, changed and charted the several patients, whose families looked up at the newcomers. It was a feeling of mutual hope and despair that spread over the room and somehow, everyone tried to smile as they made eye contact. Then the eyes went back to their loved ones and the prayers began again.

The walk to their precious daughter's bed was labored and riddled with anxiety and fear. No matter what they expected, nothing would be the same as the real thing. Her face was bruised to the point that her left eye was shut and the gashes all over her once-beautiful face were repaired with stitches and bandages. Blood was everywhere on her arms, legs and neck. Her head was covered in a white gauze bandage and her wrists bore rope marks that added to the amount of redness of their poor dear Melanie's limp body.

As she scanned her daughter on the white sheets and placed her hand in Melanie's, Abby spoke quietly so as not to disturb the others. "Is she in a coma?" Her lip quivered, not knowing what answer to anticipate.

"No ma'am. We gave her some pain medication to help her sleep and we gave her some medicine to relieve some of the swelling in her face. She will sleep most of the day."

Glenn leaned toward her face, kissed her on the nose and held her free hand. He whispered, "Honey, baby. I'm so sorry this happened to you. We'll find out who did this. I will make him pay."

"Can she hear us?" Mark questioned.

"Probably not right now, but it's good to keep talking to her. She might wake up at some point and your voices will be comforting to her."

Abby nodded. "Mommy and Daddy are here sweetheart. We love you. Mark's here too."

As he began to let his words flow, Mark broke down, "Mel, I'm sorry. I can't believe this happened to you." He turned to the doctor for answers, "Is she going to be okay? Is she going to be handicapped or anything?"

"She'll be okay, someday, and she won't be permanently disfigured or disabled. Oddly enough, she doesn't have any broken bones. She was very lucky in that capacity. Mr. and Mrs. Crawford, may I see you out in the hall?"

His voice got insistent as he saw Glenn being reluctant to leave his daughter's side. "Please." Glenn knew that voice well; it signaled bad news was coming. He was good at giving it out but getting it seemed unbelievable.

They walked into the hallway and closed the door, the doctor turned slowly and looked at Glenn. Something was wrong. "What is it?" He demanded with very little patience.

"The damage to her uterus may be unreparable. She may not be able to have children. I'm sorry." He laid his hand on Glenn's back as he excused himself to another duty. Glenn and Abby stood in apprehension as he began to think how he could tell his daughter something like this. They would wait and let the situation come as it may. The doctor did say that she "might." That seemed better than never.

Instead of going back in with Abby, he pulled out his cell phone and called his mother to let her know what had happened. He cried as he heard a busy signal. He solemnly walked back in to the ICU and padded up to Abby. She bowed her head and began to pray quietly as Mark rushed to her side and made vows to find out who did this and destroy him. The family sobbed and prayed together as the frail figure lay next to them in induced sleep. Glenn excused himself after a few minutes and decided to leave the room.

Chapter 5

Barbara sat at the phone in the den and waited for news from Glenn. The phone jolted her from her daze and she hastily reached for the phone. Breathlessly answering, "Glenn?" It wasn't her sons voice on the phone, but Jason's. He spoke without worry, "No, Ma'm. This is Jason. Is Melanie available?"

Having little tact or feeling for anyone else, she simply let him know that, "Melanie is still in the hospital. You can call back later." She hung up and didn't thing twice about what she'd said or how she'd said it. The phone rang again and she was just sure it was Jason again. Abruptly she spoke, "Now what?…Oh, Glenn honey. What is happening?"

Her son burst into tears as he stated the situation. She stood up and almost cried but the impact was more than she could handle and her legs became wobbly as she laid the phone on the desk and stared, unable to utter a word or even move.

Jason's car couldn't move quickly enough as he raced down Montclair Boulevard to the hospital. What had happened? He couldn't get to her any faster and the thoughts in his head were making him crazy. He wondered thoughts too many at a time and too difficult to comprehend. As he turned at the stoplight, he dodged a yellow Volkswagen. He didn't even notice the near miss until the barely audible honk wailed. He motioned sorry, but not really and kept going. It seemed as if the roads were never ending and the hospital kept getting farther away. He could see it in the distance but it never appeared closer. He took two more right turns and finally saw the destination he raced to.

The parking lot was full but there was an older lady walking out so he slowly paced behind her, sure that he was making her a nervous wreck. When she turned around he yelled out of the window, "Can I have your parking place?"

She felt at ease then and nodded O.K. She reached her long land barge of a car and slowly unlocked the doors. She sat down and smiled back at Jason and proceeded to put on a seat belt. She took an unreasonable amount of time in that process. He tapped his fingers anxiously on the steering wheel and sighed, as if she could hear his urgency. The brake lights finally emerged and she began the long strenuous back up. Jason wondered if this spot was really worth it. He could have parked further out and been in the hospital by now. "Oh well, it's too late. You're committed now," he thought. She was gone and he sped into the large gap he'd waited patiently on and broke out of his car with great velocity.

As he ran through the doors, he started yelling out Melanie's name looking in rooms. A security guard stopped him and grabbed him by the arms, "Son, you have to go to the desk to find someone or you'll have to leave. You're disturbing the patients." Jason apologized and asked the lady working at the information desk for her room number. He walked quickly and looked for the ICU.

His entrance was less than quiet. Abby looked up from her daze and stared into Jason's eyes. He ran over to her and tried to reach out his arms to hug her. She pushed his arms down and with a steely voice said, "I want you to walk out of here and not show your face around my daughter again."

Jason was stunned by her tone and protested, "Abby, it's me! You can't think that I did something to hurt her. I love her. Why would I do that?"

"I'll have you taken out if you don't leave on your own volition."

Glenn walked in with two cups of coffee in his hands and steadily put them on the table near the chairs. He looked in Jason's direction, "What is it you want?"

Jason didn't know how to answer. He was unaware of the whole situation. "What happened to her?" He demanded answers and he was determined not to leave until he heard the truth.

Glenn glanced at Abby and said with a puzzled look on his face,

"You don't know, do you?"

"Know what?" His eyes pleaded for their help.

"Tell him, Abby."

"Melanie was attacked last night and raped. They found her in the park this morning." Tears flooded her face as she bit her lip to keep it from quivering. Glenn's arms embraced her and he wiped her tears on his shirt. Jason's face turned pale as he lost his balance and fell backwards. The rail on the wall caught him before he made it to the floor. Glenn and Abby reached over to him and hugged him. Realizing their mistake of accusation, they sat him in a chair, fanned him and told him to relax. They promised to take him to see her when he felt a little better.

He didn't know what to think. "Wh-wh-what happened to her?" His voice stammered.

"Shhhh. Just settle down." Abby tried to console him between tears.

"She's alive. We'll see her in a bit."

That would be too long. He didn't think he could relax at all and he sat up straight, looked at Glenn and begged, "Please take me to her."

He knew it wouldn't be the same Melanie he left. "Oh, my gosh. I left her. In the park. It was my fault."

Jason, Glenn and Abby entered into the unit and Mark stood up as Jason passed him crouching near his Melanie's face. He cradled her in his arms and the tears began so heavy he couldn't control himself. Abby began to cry in Glenn's arms and they both shouldered Mark. The situation seemed so unbelievable, like a nightmare, but they knew it was real. Jason looked up and with fire in his eyes, he spoke quietly and sternly, "I'm not going to let this be the end. I'm finding the one who did this. Why? What did she do to anyone?" With that, he rose and quickly raced out of the hospital. His determination took him outside but where would he go now? He couldn't reason anything out except the need to have revenge.

Glenn asked Abby, "Maybe we should eat something. We've missed breakfast. It's almost lunchtime. I'm going to the cafeteria to get something. Mark, do you want to come?"

Abby was not thinking of food. "You two go ahead. I don't have much of an appetite. I think we should call your mother. Would you do that? Just let her know that things are going to be okay and that we'll stay here tonight. If she wants to see Melanie she can come up tomorrow when she's in her own room."

"Yes, you're right. I'll call her. I'll bring you some coffee?"

She looked at Melanie so peacefully and quietly said, "That would be fine. Oh, Glenn, make sure she called mom and dad, would you?"

After Mark and Glenn left, Abby spoke to Melanie and began to pray.

"Melanie, it's Mom. Can you hear me sweetheart? I am right here with you. I want you to know how much your family loves you. You are so special to us. I can't believe this is actually happening. Why you? Why my daughter?

"God. Oh Lord. Please hear my prayers. I ask that you heal my child. I ask that you make her strong enough to fight the emotional pain she's going to face when she wakes up. Please take away any pain she has. God, I need you to be there for this family. Be ever-present. It's a disaster and this may destroy what's left. I'm clinging on to hope. Since I accepted you in my life as my Lord and Savior, I never had a doubt that tough times would still happen. I accept that as life, but I also know that you won't give me anything more than I can handle. You know me. You know my limits. My family is so weak right now. Strengthen us. Use this to make us yours. Use me to be your tool. Save this family. Bring us back together somehow."

Glenn and Mark returned later to find Abby's head resting on Melanie's chest. Glenn tried not to startle her as he touched her shoulder, "Abby."

She raised her eyes and smiled a pitiful smile. She was worn out. Her emotions couldn't go any further. With all the drama from the night before, and then this, she could barely muster up enough energy and emotion to feel anything.

Mark spoke up, "Mom, I need to go home. I can't stay here tonight. Will you take me home or can I just take the car?"

Glenn became very put out by Mark's insensitivity. "What's the problem that you can't stay?"

Trying to keep peace in the room, Abby stood up and looked at Glenn. "Glenn, I think it's best for him to go home. He won't get a good night's sleep in one of those chairs. He's not doing anything wrong by leaving. I can drive him. I can bring us back some essentials."

The truth was that she really wanted to leave and think. The drive back would give her time to clear thoughts and regain some strength. She knew she would need it for the next round of drama, whatever that would be.

Glenn didn't seem to understand and lashed out as usual. "Why do you have to deliberately fight me on every decision I make?" The scene caused the rest of the families to look up and observe. He continued, unaware or uncaring of the audience, "Fine, take him home. I just hope your sister doesn't wake up while you're not here."

Mark turned to his mother and rolled his eyes. "I don't have to put up with this. Maybe if you'd try to be a dad once in a while and quit trying to be the lawyer of the family, we'd all get along. You treat everyone like a client. If you don't get your way, you don't take the case. Dad, you don't have a judge or jury to prove anything to. We'd all like to respect you and believe you. I'm just not sure that's what you want from us. Mom, take me home."

Abby decided to walk away in effort to keep the remainder of her dignity. Mark followed suit and Glenn sat down distraught and frustrated next to his little girl. His eyes welled up with salty water and he wondered how this could be happening.

Chapter 6

Jason sat on the floor in front of his bed and tried to gather even one clear thought. They were coming so quickly and disorganized. What else could he do? There was so much damage and he was to blame, so he reasoned.

The thoughts were broken suddenly with a hard knock on the door. "Police, we're looking for Jason Lang."

Jason picked himself off the floor and slowly sauntered to the door. He never said a word. As he opened the door to see Trigger, the campus security officer standing with a police officer, he motioned for them to enter the room. Since there was no place to sit, other than dorm beds, they chose to remain standing. The conversation began with an apology for disturbing Jason in the middle of his studies. That made him crack a laugh.

"Yeah, I was really studying hard, what with my life going so perfectly right now."

As the officer tried to move the conversation forward, he said, "Son, I'm Officer Myers. We are here to talk to you about the rape of your girlfriend, Melanie Crawford. She was found in Benchfield Park approximately 6:00 a.m. yesterday morning. Do you know anything about her being in the park the night before or who could have done this?"

"Do you think I'm a suspect, because if so, just say it!" He got frustrated and noticed Trigger eyeing the window, in a daze. Trigger couldn't care less about any of the situation but the university required a security officer to escort the police when on campus.

"You were a suspect at first, but in the ambulance, she was lucid enough to tell us you didn't do it. Someone else did it. Do you have any idea? Did she have any enemies? Anyone who might want to hurt her? Has she done something to anyone you can think of?" The questions were routine but brought about no real clues in Jason's mind. He explained the evening in little details. The party, the idiots, the argument on the way home. "She told me to stop the car and I refused. She yelled for me to stop again, and I was a fool and let her out and drove away." He remembered he didn't call her to make sure she'd gotten home. What was he thinking? He just wanted to die for his part in this. The officer then probed harder.

"Exactly where did you drop her off?"

"On the corner of Benchfield and Taylor, right in front of the fountain in the park. Where did they find her?"

"About 30 feet from the fountain."

"Was someone following us?"

The police officer started writing down in his little black notebook and looked up and said, "It's possible. Are you sure you know absolutely no one who would do this? Any lead is good enough to look into. Since you might have been followed, it might be helpful to have a list of people at the party. All of the people if you can."

"Yeah, I can get a list."

"I'll okay it with the Dean of Students, because we'll need the addresses and phone numbers of everyone at the party. We'll need it quickly. Can you have it ready by this afternoon and bring it by the station?"

Jason figured this to be the best way to make up for what happened to his sweet Melanie. "Sure."

"Mr. Lang, we appreciate your cooperation and help. That will be all. See you this afternoon." With that the officer tugged on Trigger's sleeve and woke him from his eye-open nap. With a jerk, he turned and made a beeline for the door. The policeman looked back and smirked towards Jason.

Jason sat at his desk and looked at a picture of Melanie and him. He burst into sobs and then realized he was going to get sick. He bolted for the toilet and hugged it as everything came up. When he was finished, he leaned back on the wall and buried his hands in his knees and prayed for forgiveness.

Inside the ICU, Melanie began to wake up from the medicine. She looked around puzzled, tried to speak and then fell back into sleep. The nurses ran over and called for the doctor. "Dr. Keller, the Crawford girl woke up and went back to sleep. Her heart rate is doing well, has been for the past twelve hours. She's responding well to the medications. Her swelling is going down."

Dr. Crawford was pleased with the news. "Call for recovery to get a room ready. She's going upstairs. Tell Mr. and Mrs. Crawford their daughter is doing very well by her heart rate and her brain waves look fine. She will be in her new room in about three hours. They can probably talk to her when she wakes up the next time."

Abby and Glenn were in the waiting area outside the ICU. It was the only relaxing place they had to think. The nurse approached them and gave them the information. Abby's hands grabbed Glenn's and they hugged each other, without thinking, but it felt good to both of them. "Oh, praise the Lord."

"She's still asleep now, so you probably have time to go get some clothes so you may stay overnight in her room. She's on her way to a good recovery, Mr. and Mrs. Crawford." She turned around and walked off.

Barbara sat with the phone rested between her ear and shoulder as she talked to Abby's parents. The discussion was very labored as Barbara had no intention of giving out too much information, which might prompt them to come down and stay awhile.

"So, Barbara. Can you tell us a little about her condition?" asked Sandra.

Barbara always had a smart comeback. "Well, how would I know? Nobody tells me anything. I'm supposed to be important here, but somehow, I feel like they don't want me to know. You probably know more than I do."

"Barbara, you are the only person we've had contact with. You've got to get a hold of yourself or you're going to go crazy."

Ben, in the background, had the proper time for a quick retort, "It's too late for that kind of advice, Sandra."

She shooed him away and he giggled. Sandra covered the phone and mouthed, "Ben! Watch your mouth. What if she hears you?"

"She can't hear me because she doesn't shut up long enough to hear anything. You'd better listen to her, she's still babbling." He crept away to the next room and Sandra uncovered the phone to hear,

"Do you know what I'm saying Sandra? Sandra? Did you hear me? Mark has become more than a share of problems and now that Melanie's been hurt, I'm sure that this living situation won't work much longer. Abby won't be able to see what needs to be done around here, of course she never does, but then you know that, you're her mother."

Sandra was a good holy woman and bad thoughts didn't regularly transpire so she was able to remain level headed and calm as she stated, "Barbara, I hate to cut this short, but we've got to go to the store. Would you let Glenn and Abby know that we're going to come up and we'll see them tomorrow?"

"Now that won't work. They don't need that many people around this house. It's just going to be chaos. We'll call you if there are any changes or any news."

She smiled as she ignored the protest and replied, "Okay, Barbara, see you tomorrow. Make sure you tell them. Bye Barbara." As Sandra hung up the phone, she looked at Ben and they shook their heads in disbelief.

Ben cracked one more. "Do you think it's possible to have PMS that late in life?" Sandra looked at him and rolled her eyes. "Just asking," he said. They giggled once more before Sandra sat down and let herself absorb the horrible news. Her heart was flooded with emotions allowing tears to pour over her cheeks. Ben's hand rested on her shoulder in an effort to comfort her.

"We have to get to her, Ben."

"We will. We will."

On the other end of the line, Barbara began to say something else and then realized that the phone had been hung up as a dial tone buzzed in her ear. She stared down at the phone and yelled, "Well, I never."

Mark walked through the hall and heard her statement and on his way to his room, he yelled back, "Yeah, well it's too bad your parents did!"

"You'd just better watch it young man!" She really didn't know what else to say."

Chapter 7

Jason walked into the hallway of the dorm and saw his friend, Drew. Drew was the treasurer of their fraternity. Apparently the news was all over the campus because all day long he'd been bombarded with notes on his door, phone calls that were picked up by the answering machine and the occasional pat on the back accompanied by the understanding nod.

"Hey Drew." Jason didn't sound at all like his usual upbeat self. No wonder. He looked as if a truck had run over him. But that was nothing compared to the way his Melanie looked. He couldn't close his eyes without envisioning her swollen bloody face. He couldn't shut his mind down enough to quit thinking of her.

Drew knew what had happened but the words of comfort just wouldn't come. He didn't know what to say. All he came up with was a pathetic "Jason man, I been wondering how you're doing. We heard about your girlfriend. Is she okay?"

"No she's not. She's unconscious and looks horrible. I can't believe this happened."

Still very uneasy, Drew tried to excuse himself. "Hey you take it easy. If you need anything let me know."

"Thanks man. I do need something. Can you get me a list of all the people at the party Friday night? I need their names and I'll have to get the addresses from the Dean."

"What for? I mean I can do it, but why?" Drew suddenly felt important and leaving was now on the backburner.

"The cops said they think it might have been someone who had been aware of where Mel and I were the whole night. She was being followed, they think."

"Oh my gosh! It was planned?"

"Well, I don't know how planned it was, no one knew we would have a fight that night, but it's a theory. I'll come by your room later on to see what you've got. I appreciate it."

"Are you going to the hospital?"

"Yeah, I haven't seen her today. You know if I find out who did that to her, I'll rip his head off."

Drew nodded and left the room. Jason followed him out and drove to the hospital.

At the hospital, Jason walked in much more casually than the first time. He started for the nurses' desk and asked, "Can you tell me where Melanie Crawford's parents would be? She's in ICU."

"Ms. Crawford was moved to the third floor for recovery this morning. She's in room 317. I'm sure her parents will be there. They've been staying here for the past two days. If they aren't in the room, try the cafeteria." Her smile was pleasant but didn't last long as she turned her attention to the mound of papers in front of her.

Jason faced the elevator and pressed the button up. The doors opened immediately and he stepped on and once again pressed a button. Third floor, he remembered. Recovery? Did she say recovery? He became anxious at the news. The doors flew open and he got off on the third floor. He had to choose which of two directions to go. Which way? He stared up at the walls for directions and finally found 310-330. He walked briskly and as an orderly was coming out of a room he dodged to the left and hit a patient walking her IV unit.

"Sorry, Sorry," he said and squirmed off embarrassed, but not too badly. He was on a mission. Get to Melanie and hold her. It was all he could do.

Room 317. There it was. He knocked on the door and heard Glenn. "Yes, come in."

"Glenn, hi." He didn't walk into the room until he knew he was welcome.

"Jason, come in."

"Is she awake yet?"

From the other side of the room a faint voice murmured. "Jason, I'm so sorry." SORRY? What was she sorry for? He was appalled that she was apologizing.

"No, Mel. I'm sorry. It shouldn't have happened. It shouldn't have." His hand reached for hers and he knelt down and held her. His face shared tears with hers. No one needed to blame themselves. They only needed to be together. There was no way they would let a psychotic man destroy them.

Jason looked at her and wiped a tear from her cheek. "I love you. Please forgive me."

Melanie looked at Glenn and Abby and asked, "Mom, Dad, can you leave us alone for a minute? I need to tell Jason what you just told me."

Abby looked upset and worried asking, "Are you sure you don't want us here for that?"

Glenn nodded, "Abby, let her do it. We'll be right outside in the waiting room." He patted both of their faces and they left."

Jason didn't want to know any news. It sounded like it was serious so he simply asked a barrage of questions. "How do you feel? Are you hurting right now? Do you need anything?"

Melanie smiled and knew he didn't know what else to do. "Jason, everything hurts."

"Sorry, that was a dumb thing to say."

Melanie broke into tears as she gripped Jason's hand and started to give the bad news. "The doctor told me some things I want you to know. Do you love me enough to stand with me through this?"

Jason was worried, but without hesitation, reassured her, "You know I do. What?"

"I want to hear you say that you won't leave me when you find out."

Jason couldn't imagine what could be so horrendous that she would honestly think he'd leave her. "Find out? Find out what? What are you saying?"

"The damage to my uterus was so bad, I may not be able to have children. What if I can't give you a baby? I know we'd always planned to have a family when we got married. This isn't how I planned it."

Jason looked at her in shock and then wiped a tear that streamed from her eye down her cheek. He loved her and this proved how much. Nothing aside from his relationship with Christ mattered to him as much as she did. "I know you didn't plan this. It's not your fault and maybe they will find out differently later. I will love you no matter what. Children or no children, you are what matters. The children are God's plan and things will work themselves out to His will."

"I want to believe that this had to be in God's plan but, why? How? You might never be a daddy. What kind of plan is this?"

There was about an inch of space between their faces as he tried to calm her down. "Don't forget that 'Everything works together for the good to those who trust in Him.' How do you think we made it this far together? Melanie, we can get through this. Please trust me. I'm going to find whoever did this and he will be punished. The police think it was someone who knew where you were that night. They think we were being followed. Have you made any statements?"

"No. I didn't make any statements because I can't remember anything. I can't remember any of it. I woke up here. I haven't even seen what I look like."

"Why not?"

Melanie put her face down so as to hide her face and shrugged. "Nobody had handed me a mirror. Do I look that disgusting?"

Jason put his hand on her chin and raised her face so he could see her eyes. She was so beautiful to him. He loved her and nothing would change that. "You just look hurt. You'll always be beautiful."

"Will you hand me a mirror?"

Jason knew how to joke with her. "Are you sure? You're not going to hit me for lying are you?"

Obviously this time his joking was untimely. "I do look gross!" She fell apart in his arms as he grasped her and he held her tightly kicking himself inside for the stupid remark.

He tried to erase the moment and smirked, "I'm only kidding. You will be a little shocked but you don't look gross." He got up from the bed and walked around her and handed over the mirror. They looked in the reflection together. He smiled gently but noticed her face looked distressed at the image looking back at her.

Her fingers rolled gently over the cuts, bruises and swelling. She looked at Jason in the mirror and her eyes pleaded for him to help her.

Jason held her and they wept together. "I will. I will. You aren't going to go through this alone. I promise."

The door opened and the Crawfords followed Dr. Keller in. Jason and Melanie looked up and listened as the doctor began. "Melanie, your HIV tests came back negative and your heart rate is normal. Your stitches look good. You're well on your way to a full recovery. We will know more about your possibility of children after your wounds heal but don't let that be a big issue right now. I think you can go home tomorrow. I would like to have you tested for HIV and STDs regularly. The nurse will go over that with you when you're discharged and we will want to see you for a follow-up visit to check your wounds."

Melanie mumbled, "These aren't the wounds I'm worried about." Remembering the possible life-changing news that she'd just told Jason.

"Melanie, you can't dwell on the bad news, that will only prolong the healing process. You've got to keep an optimistic view on things. Now family will need to keep things calm, tidy and easy for her for the next few weeks. She'll need to be in a good, healthy environment. I'll check on you tomorrow morning before we let you go. You should get a good night's sleep. Your pain medication will help you rest." He excused himself and they all stood near Melanie and as hands stretched around the bed, Abby started in prayer. Tears were shed as they all asked God to heal and give peace.

When they were done, Glenn quickly let go of Abby's hand and stated, "I guess I should call Mother and let her know she's coming home tomorrow."

Abby interjected, "Yes, and have her call my parents too."

Chapter 8

Later that afternoon, Jason made his way back to the dorm and took double steps to the third floor. He knocked on Drew's door and heard him say, "Yeah, come in."

Drew looked up from some books and saw Jason standing there in the doorway. "Hey, I got that list of people at the party for you. Some of the addresses aren't on there. Jake helped me get it together. We tried to figure out about how many people were there and we got a lot of numbers for you."

Jason grabbed the list and scanned it hoping to see something stand out in bold or red but everything was normal. Nothing stood out to him. "Thanks so much. I don't even know where to begin. I guess I should let the cops do the work, right?"

He nodded at Drew once more and walked out into the hall. As he looked at the list again, he tried to focus as his eyes began to water. He picked up his face and made his way for the police station.

As Jason walked the opposite direction, a male in nondescript clothing stood at the end of the hallway. His face snarled into a grin. The hate inside him fed off the energy that Jason emitted. With pride the stranger muttered, "I got her first."

He cackled and then turned around and strolled away. Nobody noticed him at all. He was the face in the crowd and he was anonymous.

Jason entered through the doors of the police station and felt like he'd walked into a foreign country. The front desk was off to the right of the door and the officer sitting behind it looked to be about his age. "Hi, my name is Jason Lang. I'm here to see Officer Myers."

Myers noticed him walk through the doors and he made his way over to him. "Mr. Lang, good to see you. Did you bring it?"

"Yes sir, a friend put it together. These are about all the people we think were at the party. I hope it helps. Some of the addresses aren't there."

"That's okay. When we question some of them, we'll put everything together. I appreciate this. Hopefully we can get a suspect from it. Have you seen your girlfriend? How is she?"

"They put her in her own room and she's going home tomorrow. She's not able to have children." The lump in his throat became a warning that it was time to go. "Well, I'd better get, but please let me know if you need anything or if something pops up."

Myers nodded and held out his hand. "Sure, I'll be in touch."

As Jason walked out to his car and started to remember the party, one specific scene wouldn't leave his head.

"Melanie, Do you want something to drink?"

"Yeah. I think I'll have a glass of Coke."

"Okay, I'll be right back."

Melanie sat and waited and waited. She saw Jason and his friends acting stupid and got angry. She walked up to him and stared until she got his full attention. He was supposed to know what she thought, and in most cases, he honestly did. Of course, he did. She hated those parties.

"Long journey for just a Coke," she teased with a touch of nerve.

"Oh yeah, here. Sorry." He kissed her on the cheek.

Melanie wasn't happy with that. "Jason, I'm ready to go. Can you pry yourself away?"

Jason protested and smiled, "Not yet, Mel, just hold on fifteen more minutes."

Melanie pouted, "Oh fine!" She turned and walked away. Jason saw someone's back behind a post and he seemed to be going the same direction as Melanie. He couldn't figure out who because of the darkness.

The scene was vivid in his memory and he began to talk to himself out loud in the car. "Who is that guy? I wonder if that's him?"

Chapter 9

With anticipation and relief the Crawfords pulled into their driveway with their daughter. Oddly, they noticed Ben and Sandra's car in the driveway. Abby's face lit up and she looked at Glenn, "Oh my gosh. Mom and Dad drove all the way here."

Glenn smiled with joy for her. Mark helped Melanie out of the car and the grandparents came wandering out on the front porch. Sure enough. Ben and Sandra were there. Glenn worried about the new dynamics that the house would take on with the whole family there.

"Mom didn't say anything about them coming. I wonder why she didn't tell us," he quietly mumbled to Abby. His eyes widened and expressed a true feeling of pleasure as his outstretched hand grasped Ben's. "Ben, Sandra. It's great to see you." He hugged them both and remembered how it felt to be a family with them. He loved their visits, though infrequent that they were. They welcomed him into the family from day one and he couldn't have been more blessed.

"We're so surprised you're here."

They all shot a momentary look at each other as they realized how it became a surprise.

Ben glanced at Sandra and then at Barbara. She cunningly smiled it off and said, "Oh, I forgot to mention that they were coming to stay for a while. I explained that we really didn't have any need for them to be here, but you know."

Glenn was used to his mother's abrupt and crude words but he wouldn't accept that with his in-laws. "Mom, that's rude. We're so glad you came. Melanie will have a great time recuperating with you around. Let's get in the house."

Abby picked up Melanie's little bag of hospital items. "Melanie, I'll get your bags and take them to your room. Do you want to sit with us in the den or would you like to rest for a while?"

Melanie didn't like to be doted on so she quickly exclaimed, "I will be fine wherever people are. Mamaw, Papaw, I have missed you so much. Thank you for coming up. It means a lot to me." She wanted to hug them both so badly but the pain was too bad that she just patted them on the backs. They understood. Barbara stood off to the side and watched as they got special treatment. She resented them but deep down, she knew she had only herself to blame. She'd pushed so many people away with her bitter thoughts. How could she ever become something she wasn't? She'd always been that way.

The reunion continued in the house. The stately clock in the foyer struck two o'clock p.m. Ben had been waiting to see his baby Melanie since five that morning. They arrived early, which meant they drove all night long. Everyone was exhausted but their emotions were running so high they didn't seem to notice.

"Sweetheart, are you feeling better? Mamaw and I are so sorry this happened to you. I wish I could do something for you."

"You came to see me and I couldn't be more grateful." A smile emerged from under the scabs and bandages. He could see the apparent smile in her eyes rather than her mouth.

"Oh, my sweet girl." Sandra's composure faded and she began to cry while she clutched Melanie's hand tightly in hers.

"I'm okay. I'll be fine. I just need to get this whole thing out of my mind. Move on with life." Melanie protested sternly.

Barbara, feeling quite out of place, jumped in with a quick unemotional retort, "That's right, honey. Life doesn't stop when tragedy strikes. You just have to plug on." Everyone glanced around to see the others' reactions and thought just about the same thing; how inappropriate Barbara could be.

"Well, it will take some time, Mother. Melanie's strong, but she needs to feel like she's emotionally ready to start again. She may stay out of school for a while. I think she needs to take a break away from things."

"Oh, honey, if you baby her like that, she's just never going to put it behind her. Let her forget."

Melanie watched the unbelievable tennis match over her health issues and jumped in, "I'm right here. I can make up my own mind about these things. I'm fine. The damage is only physical." Melanie's privacy had been invaded and everyone knew what was best for her, or so they thought. She couldn't forget anything but at the same time, was totally unable to remember the situation.

Eyes met again and Melanie noticed the apprehension of her words on her family's ears. She knew she was unable to disassociate herself from what happened.

Abby broke the silence, "Well, let's go in and have some lunch." She walked over to Ben and Sandra and embraced them one more time, whispering, "Mom, Daddy, I am so happy you came. Barbara didn't tell us you were coming."

Ben whispered back with a wink, "Not surprising."

Sandra popped him on the shoulder, "Ben, you'd better watch your step around here. She lives here and we are guests."

Abby smirked and quietly replied, "Funny you'd mention that, Daddy." With a turn of her heel she made her short journey to the front door as Ben and Sandra stood confused looking at each other. What kind of remark was that?

Not long after the family reunion began, the doorbell chimed announcing a new visitor. Ben headed for the door and looked through the peephole. Swinging the door open, he smiled, "Jason Lang, what a great surprise. Come in. Come in. Melanie's in the living room with everyone."

With a slow movement to the living room Ben continued with small talk as he placed his hand on Jason's shoulder. "How are you and your studies?"

"I'm fine, sir. How are you and Mrs. Palmer? I'm glad you came down to see Melanie."

"Yes, siree, we're doing fine." He stopped and pulled Jason back by the elbow just before they reached the threshold of the room, "Jason, do you know who could have done this? My baby deserves answers. I don't know if relying on the police is going to get results. They may be good but I think the best investigators are those who really care about the victim. The pursuit is relentless when it's done by someone in love." Jason knew he had to continue to search for the answers and Ben gave him the confidence to know that he would complete the mission.

"The police asked me to help them get a list of all the people who were at the party the night she was attacked. I gave a really long bunch of names, but who knows what will happen. It's just so hard to see her looking the way she does. I know it must hurt so badly. She saw herself in the mirror for the first time yesterday. It was so pitiful. She was in shock. I don't know if she was expecting to look that bad. How is she? Is she doing all right today?"

"She acts like nothing is wrong. Like nothing happened. She's trying to hide from reality. She could use a good time with you right now. Let's go in and you can rescue her from us old fogies who keep telling her that she needs to get some rest."

They walked into the den and Melanie's eyes lit up at the sight of Jason. She tried to stand up but he caught her and set her back on the sofa. "Hey sweetie." Kissing her cheek they seemed to disappear from the rest of the group. "How are you?"

"I'm doing fine. I didn't expect to see you here tonight. Don't you have a test to study for?"

Jason grimaced, "Some things can wait. Others are just more important."

"Why thank you, sir. Would you like some iced tea?"

He declined and Sandra rose to hug him, "Jason, I'm so glad you came over. You look wonderful. Doesn't he look wonderful? Is college being good to you?"

"Yes m'am. I decided my major would be in Christian Ministry and Psychology. I guess the two can go hand in hand, huh?"

Melanie, popped in, "He's got a test in History tomorrow. I think he can do it just fine, but this professor he's got seems to put the pressure on him. It really rattles him."

Sandra smiled. "I'm sure your grades are good. You always seemed so smart and studious. You'll be perfect in the ministry. Good to know some people are on our side since most are always working against us."

His smile showed gratitude for the encouragement. He looked over at Melanie and attempted to start a conversation. "So how do you feel, Mel?"

She got defensive, "I said I'm fine. Let's quit talking about this. Change the subject. Don't bring it back up."

Barbara just didn't get it. "Well, amen. I'm not going let this incident spoil our family get-together."

Abby mentioned out loud, "The incident is the reason we are having this get-together. It's hardly spoiling us. It could, however, make us closer."

Glenn hated the conflicts at home, mostly because he dealt with so many conflicts at the office. "You two. Well, I say we all go out and get something to eat. Pizza? What do you say?"

Everyone stood up and Melanie struggled to rise with Jason's help. To keep it light, Ben piped in, "Great. I'm starving. Sandra, honey, would you mind getting my keys? We can take our car with two more people. Glenn, Abby?"

"Sure." Glenn didn't hesitate.

Mark escorted his Mamaw and Papaw outside and had some explaining to do. "Mark, what did you do to your hair?"

He laughed and replied, "Mamaw, I'm growing my hair out just for you. I know how you like long hair."

Sandra loved him so much and they communicated more like friends than relatives. "Oh, brother." She rolled her eyes and they went arm in arm to the car.

Barbara stood in between the cars and wondered which car she was to ride in. Abruptly and without caution, she exclaimed, "I still don't have a ride!"

Glenn looked up from the back seat and said, "Okay, Mark, you take Grandma in your truck."

"Dad?!"

Barbara knew she was unwanted at the moment, "No, that's okay. I just won't go."

Glenn didn't want to seem cold, "Mom, you can ride with me,

and Mark can go with Abby and her parents." Mark smiled and jumped into the back seat as his father got out on the other side and caught the truck keys that were flung at him. "Come on, Mom."

Upon returning from the pizza place, the cars seemed weighted down and there were many moans and groans as they tried to pull themselves out after the heavy meal of pizza and breadsticks. Jason and Melanie stayed in the car for a few minutes extra.

He knew it would hit a nerve, but he asked anyway, "Are you going to sleep all right tonight? Are you scared?"

"Jason, it's over. I'm fine. Nothing is going to happen to me. Drop it. It makes me mad that nobody will quit talking about it. Don't get on my bad list. I'll kiss you with my bloody, scabby lip." They both cringed. "Oh, that was gross. Sorry." She hid the fear and pain well but mostly for herself. Nobody really bought her courage. They knew if the situation were reversed, they would be terrified to close their eyes, to walk to a room alone, to hear the phone ring, anything. It was normal to be frightened and they were going to allow her all the time she needed, although she protested she needed no time.

She smiled back at him and he put his finger on her mouth. "Well, I love you in spite of your scabby lip. Even your puffy eye doesn't bother me." He kissed her on the forehead and she leaned into his shoulder as he held her close and stroked her long, luminous blonde hair.

Melanie leaned back and looked at the ground, ashamed. "What about the children factor?"

"Don't worry about that. You can't change that, and frankly if you could I don't think we could test how strong our love is. It's stronger than steel, baby. You're not getting rid of me."

Melanie's eyes filled with tears and her lips produced a smile that seemed innocent and secure. "I love you." She leaned over and kissed him. "Now go home and study. Do well on your exam. We need you to pass that course."

As she started out of the car, Jason's hand grabbed her and pulled her back. "Wait, before you go, I need your help. The police asked me to help find out who did this to you. They think it was someone at the party. I was remembering..."

She jerked her hand away and her eyes frowned as she remarked, "I said forget it. Quit bringing it up! I just want to forget anything ever happened. Will you at least let me do that?"

"Mel, he could do this again, maybe not to you but to someone else. Help me, if not for yourself, then for another girl."

Melanie gave the shy smile that said she was terrified but unable to be real about it. "No. He's gone. It's nothing to dwell on. Call me after your test. Goodnight."

She shut the car door, and Jason watched her walk to the door and get in safely. It was his mission to be her keeper now. She made the walk with a knot in her stomach, but her desire to bring back normalcy was stronger so the walk, though laborious and fearful, was made. It seemed a mile away to the door and her stomach led up to her throat.

She thought the pizza would come up if the door to the house didn't get closer. When she made it inside, the whole family, minus one Barbara, was in the kitchen watching her and the concern on their faces made her annoyed.

"What? I didn't get attacked on the way in. Why are you looking at me this way?" Being on the defensive, even when they had said nothing was her best way to fight the feeling of terror inside her. She left the room and started to turn around to apologize when a memory flashed through her head. The scene showed her hearing a voice and seeing a mask. She also heard him say he saw her at the party. In terror, she quickly went back into the kitchen and apologized for the previous remarks and continued with, "I'm tired. I think I'll go to bed. See you all in the morning." Her voice was shaky and her face pale. The family looked at each other and Abby stood up to walk towards her.

"Do you want me to come up there with you, Sweetie?" She hoped for an open invitation but accepted the reply.

"I think I can get to my room without being attacked, unless Grandma's in the hall." Everyone snickered a little and Glenn frowned. They got the message.

"Mel, you'd better watch what you say about my mom. Let's give her a break now, huh?" He hugged her and she suddenly felt a little sorry. Mostly she felt sorry that the remarks had hurt her dad.

Melanie's grasp on her father got stronger and she felt comfort, safety and for the first time in days, a little relaxed. He noticed her grip tighten on him and he let the bond continue as long as it would. Suddenly fearing her strong demeanor be torn away, she let go and her body stiffened again as she excused herself. "Sorry Dad. I'll try to be nicer to Grandma. Goodnight everyone. See you in the morning."

Melanie made slow tracks to the hallway and up the stairs. It was dark so she flipped the light on to lead the way to her room. Even the glow of the hall light didn't make it easier to walk into the room alone. She kept telling herself that it was fine and nothing was there. She even started to believe it a little. Her room got closer and then she stepped over the threshold to look in and see that everything was normal and nothing had changed. Her pile of crumpled clothes that she'd promised to pick up were still hanging on the chair and her bed was still unmade. Apparently they had been more concerned with other things than the appearance of her room. The thought of that made her satisfied.

Downstairs, the family mulled over the reactions that Melanie had when anyone even brought up the rape or her feelings. "Doesn't it seem like she's denying that anything even happened? She's trying to make herself believe that it's over." Abby spoke up.

Glenn looked worried and said, "Well, she'll have to accept it and face the demon someday. I feel so helpless. I'm an attorney and I can't seem to do anything to get the guy who hurt her. I couldn't protect my baby girl." Abby reached over and put her hand on his knee as they both sat at the counter. He put his hand on hers and she smiled a faint smile that told him she needed him. The language was opening up.

Ben interjected, "Glenn, you can't take responsibility for something like this. It's a freak thing that happened and no one could have seen it coming. God will take care of the rest. You have to believe that."

Melanie stood looking vacantly around her room for a long period of time. The phone rang. She just knew it was Jason calling to tell her good night. She yelled to the family downstairs, "I'll get it! Hello." There was no answer. "Jason?" Fear paralyzed her and her heart pounded as if she were going to explode. She timidly said one more time, "Hello, who is this?" She didn't really want to know.

The distorted metallic voice sounded familiar, "I see you got out of the hospital. You look bad girl, really bad. I hope I didn't hurt you too much. The nurses were nice to you. I could tell by the way they would smile at you. You seemed to perk up when they were around. But even with a pretty smile, you might want to warn people you look at. You could really scare a person with that face. I have another mask if you'd like to borrow it. Oh, by the way. I used gloves so the mask they retrieved won't be traced back to me. They have no leads. None. Pretty girl, you are all mine and no one..."

She slammed the phone down and struggled through fear and pain to cross the hall to take a shower. It was the only place she could think of that would allow her to wash off the dirt and filth that the stranger had left on her. She got in the streaming water and cried aloud knowing that no one could hear her.

The prayers came flowing like the water. "Lord, I am so scared and you are the only one who can take the fear away. I gave my life to you and you saved me. But this time, I need you to save me from the monsters. I am so scared. I can't admit it to anyone but you and you are the only one who can fix this. Why did you let this happen? Where were you? Why didn't you come? Heal me. Make it go away. Make him go away."

Chapter 10

The house seemed to bustle and the noises were familiar. Finally a day she felt like everything might be normal again. Loud music roared from Mark's closed door. She didn't mind, but had to be a big sister and at least let him know that she was still older than he.

"Mark! Turn that down! I can't sleep."

The music got quiet and Mark walked into her room. "Sorry. You sleep well? I didn't. Grandma-who-never-shuts-up had to sleep on the floor in my room. Mom gave her room to Mamaw and Papaw. I hope they disinfected her sheets before they laid down in them." They both grinned and then Melanie remembered her promise to her father. "We'd better watch that kind of talk. Dad's serious," she said.

Melanie sat up in her bed and finally answered his first question. "I slept okay after I took one of my pain pills. They seem to put me out for a good while. Did Grandma keep talking?"

Mark rolled his eyes and replied, "No, snoring, wheezing, coughing, hacking; every noise abnormal to fall asleep. Her talking would probably have been easier to take." He thought about what he said and they both looked at each other crookedly. "Nah!" they resounded in stereo.

Melanie was very protective of her brother and he was very protective of her. They grew up with a great respect for each other and the two could always kid around, even to the point that others were sure they would kill each other one day. NO chance of that. They loved each other and the bond grew closer every year. The rape was bound to draw them closer still. Melanie knew she could trust her brother. There was no question that if she requested something, he would come through for her.

Melanie looked at him seriously and he wondered what was so secretive. "Would you do something for me? You have to promise not to tell Mom and Dad, or anyone."

Mark was confused at the request, "What?" He had a feeling he would regret what he was doing.

Melanie got up from her bed, sauntered to the door and quietly closed it. She turned around still tightly holding onto the doorknob for security. "Promise! You can't tell Mom and Dad. I'll kill you if you do."

Mark giggled at her demand, "Well, I know *that* isn't true. What's going on?" His face transformed into a frown knowing that this couldn't be good.

She proceeded to tell him, "Last night when the phone rang and I got it, I thought it was Jason, but nobody answered when I said Hello. I stayed on the line and the guy was there."

Mark's face was angry and he didn't know how to react, so he pried for more information just to give himself time to register the news. What more could this guy do? "The guy who…oh, my gosh! What did you do? What'd he say to you?" His rage grew even more intense and he was close to blowing his cool.

Melanie tried to calm him down a little but it wouldn't work and she knew it. "He told me I looked bad, just stuff like that. He said he could see me in the hospital. He was there."

"Why won't you tell Mom or Dad? Mel, you have to. He's stalking you!"

Melanie gripped his arm and her eyes looked scared as she begged, "You promised, Mark. Don't say anything about it. I figure he's just trying to get me mental."

He gave in reluctantly with a sigh, "What do you want me to do?"

Melanie leaned against her dresser and stared at the ground, bit her lower lip and then looked up at him. "If the phone rings, would you answer it? Let me know if it's anything weird."

"Weird, Mel? It's perverted. If he's calling you, he knows who you are, where you live and when you leave. I don't know, Mel. You really aren't being safe. You could be attacked again. He's a monster."

"I know, but I just want to forget the whole incident. By not bringing it up and not bringing attention to myself, I intend to put it all behind me."

"You won't be able do that if he keeps calling you. And what if he..."

She quickly interrupted him, "No, there are no what ifs. None, Mark. I mean it, you can't let me down." She walked into the hallway leaving Mark behind in her bedroom. She turned around and mouthed to him, "Remember, you promised!"

He realized that he never really made the promise, but he wouldn't betray her. He did resolve to tell Jason, however.

Mark looked around the room for something, anything to throw that wouldn't really break or create cause for stirring downstairs. He lifted one of her stuffed animals and pelted it across the room. He never imagined in a million years that secrets of this magnitude would be the bond that he and his sister would share. His hand felt her pillow and then he knew that her safety was more important than anything. Mark's loyalty to his sister was being compromised by the urge to do the safe thing. He remembered her pleas for him to promise that he would tell no one. Only one thing mattered, he wanted her to feel safe. He would manage to fulfill that promise. "Man! Who are you, sick freak?"

Chapter 11

The light blinked repeatedly until the finger reached out to hear the message. Actually it appeared that there were four new messages. Mark held his breath anticipating the first message and prayed it was just the usual neighbor, or call from one of Dad's clients.

Message 1: Melanie, I heard about the bad news. Sorry you can't have children. I guess it's best. They would all be like you, a fake, a clown. Call me.

Message 2: Melanie Dear, you haven't been around your house today. I wonder where you are? Seeking shelter? My but aren't you the shy one. You weren't so shy the other night. Talk to you later. Allrighty, Bye, Bye.

Message 3: Mel! Why are you not answering? I guess I should have expected you to be away. There are too many mirrors in that house, huh? Can't stand to look at yourself? I can't stand to look at you either. I wonder what other people think? The mask sure suited you. Made you who you really are, a liar, a phony.

Message 4: Melanie, this is getting old. I'm tired of talking to this machine. Pick up the phone! And by the way, I *will* hurt you if you ever betray my trust again. I thought we had something special going on here. You even answered my call last night. What's wrong? I'll call you later on tonight. You'd better be there. By the way, I can see your room from where I am right now. Surprise, you're on candid camera.

Mark listened to the metallic voice over again and wondered what sick man could come up with the words that generated from this mind. Not willing to take his vow to his sister lightly, he lifted the tape out of the player and replaced it with another from the hall desk.

Barbara opened the front door with no grace and looking frustrated with a bag of groceries in her arms. She glared at Mark and noticed him replacing the tape. With suspicion that he was hiding one of his many sins, she questioned, "Any messages for me?"

Mark smarted back, "Are there ever any messages for you?"

Barbara's mouth pursed and the frown was definitely a comment to Mark that he was not on her good children list. "There is another bag of groceries in the car, go get 'em."

Mark decided to be of assistance to her for once, so he went out to the car to get the rest of the bags. Jason's car pulled into the drive. He was bringing Melanie back home from school. Mark waved to them and started to move towards the red car. Inside, Barbara got a tad bit nosey and pushed play to hear the messages, the new tape was completely blank. She hit the table with her fist and murmured, "That kid is so rotten." She turned and looked out the door to make sure he was obeying her command to get the groceries inside. Seeing him leaning on Jason's car, Barbara reminded him of the reason he was out there. Mark's eyes rolled in abhorrence as he brooded all the way back to the car. He picked up a bag, the light one, and figured that would settle her down. As usual, he was completely mistaken.

"Uh, huh. That is the lightest bag. You can lift more than that." Her brassy voice resonated through the neighborhood so in order to calm any scene that she frequently made, he turned and gathered up one more bag. With the tape still in his pocket, his main goal was to get back out to talk to Jason. He went through his promise in his head, one more time for clear understanding. His vow was that he wouldn't tell Mom and Dad, not Jason.

Mark laid the bags on the kitchen table and scooted out before he could receive another assignment. Jason was dropping Melanie off after school. The chit-chat that was going on in the car would soon be interrupted by the little brother. Melanie slowly pulled herself out of the little sports car. It was difficult because it sat so low she felt as if she would be better having pulleys attached to hoist her out. Still in pain, she winced and both guys lunged out of concern. "I'm fine." She left the car door open and when she made it into the house, Mark plopped down in the passenger seat. Pulling out the tape, he pushed it into Jason's hand and told him to listen to it when he got a chance. "If you're trying to find who raped her, use this. She doesn't know it came today but do what you can with it. It was on our answering machine. He called her last night, too. Did she tell you that?"

Jason's face looked more like a bounty hunter on a mission than a youth minister. "No, she neglected to tell me. Did she say anything to him?"

"He said he could see her from where he was. That freaked her out and she has made me promise to keep quiet to Mom and Dad. I think that's a horrible idea."

Jason pushed the tape into his cassette player and awaited the evil voice that would proceed. Each message made him realize that this was someone who knew her and could follow her, and he couldn't imagine anyone that she knew that would be capable of something this disturbing. The front door closed and they looked up as Melanie was on her way back to the car. Jason's quick hand pulled the tape and he pressed it up under his seat. She never knew.

Mark stood up out of the car and he said, "Hey, when you want to do that, man let me know. I'd love to." Passing her, he motioned at the chauffer and smiled as he said, "Your chariot awaits, My Lady."

She smirked and grabbed his arm pressing him for information. "You didn't say anything to mom or dad did you? Did he call again?"

Mark was vague and proud of his mental reasoning for doing what he'd done. "No and Yes. I'll tell you later." Her face went confused and he quickly turned and went inside to avoid any more conversation. His heart finally rested when he got inside the doors. Not too long after he was calmed down, SHE came in with orders and demands. He tried so hard to tune her out but that voice, and that tone, it wasn't deafening, though most of the time he wished it was. To keep some peace, since the household had been turned upside down the past few days, he obeyed. Barbara stood incredulous as she watched him do as he was told. The key was that he was told, never respectfully asked or requested to help. She just assumed a command would work better. In this case, it was working. However this would be the only time he ever gave in and probably the last, until the attitude of one loud grandmother changed.

Jason tried to look as nonchalant as possible when Melanie got back in the car. "Hey, Mel, I was thinking we could go over to the dorm for a while so I can finish some laundry. Is that okay?"

Melanie nodded without dreading the evening plans. She felt safe, secure, unseen with Jason. What could happen with him present? Her mind deviated to the horrible night. She couldn't close off the thoughts and though Jason was gabbing to her about some song on the radio, she visualized the look on his face with the horrible clown mask. She saw his eyes, cold and with complete disgust towards her. What had she done to him? Who was he? The questions began to speak over one another as the voice in her head grew louder and more jumbled.

"Is that okay? Mel? Are you listening to me?"

Melanie jerked from the visions in her mind and turned to Jason. "What?"

"I asked if you wanted to wash my laundry for me?" He grinned, but he noticed how pallid her face appeared. He thought to himself, *Something is going on in that head of yours. Why won't you let me in?*

"Yeah, you've got nerve. I'm not doing your dirty clothes. But, if you're really nice to me, I'll fold them for you. Deal?"

He giggled. "Oh, the thrill of domestic work."

Saturday arrived the next morning and Jason's laundry was far from being finished or even sorted correctly. After a quick call to Melanie, he jumped in his car, picked her up for bagels and a great cup of latte. Conversation was light and beautiful, just like it always had been. Melanie kept her mind clear and concentrated on the precious man who sat across from her at the coffee shop. It was almost like old times but something began to gnaw at her inside. She was becoming calloused. She couldn't tell what she was getting cold to, but it was certainly rising in her heart. They finished the simple breakfast time and left to complete Jason's loads of laundry at his dorm room.

The car ride ended and they made their way up to his dorm room to get his mountain of laundry that seemed to have exploded around his room. Some of it wasn't Jason's, but his roommate didn't seem to care if it all got jumbled together. Toby would think that if it got into the pile of laundry, it would get washed someday. It would, since neither Melanie nor Jason was really willing to spend the time to mull through it all. Jason gathered it all into his laundry bag and left the room, leaving Melanie in there completely alone. He realized what he'd done within a few seconds. He sprinted back down the hall and ran into his room to make sure she was okay. "Lock the door after me. Don't let anyone in, except me of course." He felt secure in telling her how to stay safe. But she didn't really feel safe anywhere if he wasn't there.

Melanie parked herself on the chair in front of Jason's desk, then developed more and more fear. Her heart would feel like skipping beats as her breath was nearly muzzled. She tried to remain calm as the time went by that he was putting whites in with bleach and colors with like colors. She stopped her mind for a moment and spoke as if to another person, *Melanie, you have got to stop thinking like this. You are fine and you are safe.* She told herself this persistently until Jason rapped on his door. It startled her out of her trance but she felt relief when she heard the comforting voice speak, "Mel, it's me."

As she opened the door there stood her knight as she grabbed his arm. This was the first time since she'd gotten released from the hospital that she had displayed any sort of emotion that resembled fear. He wondered if she was finally able to let go of being so strong and he wanted so much for her to need him. He decided to open the can of worms. "How are you doing? Are you having any nightmares? 'Cause if you are, you can lay it on me. I can help you, even if I just listen."

Melanie decided to blow his concern off, although deep down, she wanted to let it all out. It was only time that would bring the volcano into life.

"The whole thing is a nightmare. My hair looked so much better last year. Don't you think so? It had a lot more shape to it." She was holding up a picture of herself and trying to force the conversation to stay light, meaningless and without stress.

He grabbed the picture out of her hand and placed it face down on the desk. Cupping her face in his gentle hands, Jason pressed the issue further, "Why? Why are you so afraid to talk about this? Why won't you let me help you? You're being so pig-headed. I love you and I know he hurt you, more ways than one. But, you can't shut me out. We are going through this together. You may think it's just you, all about you, but I feel something too. I feel like it's my fault. Like you could've been safe from this if I hadn't been so careless. I lost something too. You are going to be my wife someday and it's my child that you can't ever have. How does that make me feel? Maybe you think I'm being selfish, maybe I am in a way, but Mel, you are everything in the world to me and I can't help you because you won't let me in."

Tears would not stop as they clung to each other and found solace in the warmth that they created together. Finally, the lava started to flow and she pulled away in order to face him and look into his eyes.

"I am so scared. Jason, I am sorry that you are left out of this. I sure want you there but you can't possibly know what it feels like to know that the things I'd saved for you and our marriage are gone. Do you know what it's like to have your skin torn to shreds, screaming and crying for help and no one hearing you? I cried myself to sleep tied to a tree and naked. Some man I don't even know found me like that. It's not only painful, but shameful. It's embarrassing and humiliating. I have no idea what I did to get into that situation, but the truth is, I'd like to forget it. I try to sleep at night and I see his mask in my face, feel his hands tearing me apart, hitting me and I can't fight him. I don't scream because I can't wake my family. I can't forget and I can't close my eyes because it replays over and over. Don't expect me to be so anxious to give in to my feelings and share them."

"Please, Mel. You're not going to be able to carry all of this yourself and I can't help you deal with it without knowing you can come to me and unload. If you won't talk to me, please promise me that you are laying it all at God's feet."

As the whites of her eyes rolled down at the floor, she couldn't help but disagree. God, why would she even lay it at *His* feet? He wasn't watching over her that night so she was positive He wouldn't be there now that the excitement was over. The argument that would ensue if she told Jason how she really felt, it just wasn't worth it. She would have to take the wall down in order for their relationship to survive through the bitter circumstances that had occurred.

Swallowing her pride she hugged Jason and then pulled away, with her arms crossed over her chest for security. She began to let him into her terrifying world. "You're right, I have to tell you, Jason. He knows where I live and he's called me. Only once that I know of. I told Mark. He said he's going to answer the phone from now on. I made him promise not to tell anyone." The corner of her lip curled as her teeth lightly bit down awaiting his response.

The bombshell she thought she'd thrown at him wasn't quite the shocker that she thought it would be. His eyes tried to look surprised but since he'd already spoken to Mark, she could tell he knew something.

"What?" Her voice coerced for an answer. They jerked simultaneously at the clanging ring of the telephone.

Jason picked up and glanced at Melanie as he listened to Officer Myers. Melanie only picked up a few pieces of the conversation but it was enough to tell her it was about her. As she had suspected, Jason spoke slowly, "Yes, Officer. I have Melanie right here, let me ask her to talk to you."

She was terribly reluctant but took the phone anyway. "Yes?"

Officer Myers' voice sounded official and serious, "Melanie, I would like you to come down to the station and do a line up for us. There was another rape two nights ago and we caught the guy. See if he may be the same one who attacked you. That will make two charges of rape and assault. The jury would find it easier to put him away if there are two testimonies."

Fear struck her in the heart and again her pulse began to press harder and harder till she thought she would burst. "NO! I don't want to see him again. I don't want to. Jason?" She pleaded at him for help. He was on the other side of the coin and wouldn't answer her.

Officer Myers voice sounded again with a bit more urgency and sympathy. "I understand your fear, but I ask you to see the importance of this."

She hesitated and then with a long sigh proceeded to give in to the law. "I don't want to, but I will. He won't know I'm there, will he?" Jason stood up and put his hands on her shoulders from behind. She felt safer with him there.

"No, you'll be safe. And if this is the guy who raped you, then we'll have him in custody and you can't be reached from the jail. We can get you to the lineup when you come in. I appreciate this." He hung up but she stood with the phone to her ear. Jason turned her around and looked into her eyes. They were glassy and she was still. He knew that she was terrified. His arms pulled her to him and he proceeded to pray out loud.

"Lord, you are so present in our lives and right now, Melanie may feel like she is completely alone. Please give her rest, peace and strength for the road that is set before us. She's afraid, so am I Lord, and I place this in your hands. Lead us to a place of quiet solitude knowing that you love us and protect us."

Melanie pulled away and with tears in her eyes, turned and faced the wall. He'd never seen her pray this way before. She wasn't praying. Her mouth opened and repeated the last line of the prayer. "Knowing that you love and protect us? I can't believe that right now, Jason. He didn't protect me. He let me lay in a bush while some freak did horrible things to me. He let me lay there passed out, naked and cold while joggers passed me in the park. He didn't protect me. Please don't push this with me."

Shock was setting in as he tried to digest the words of betrayal from Melanie's mouth. He couldn't fathom her hatred of her Savior.

All of a sudden, it was Jason in a room with a stranger. She knew she hurt him with her words and couldn't face him. She couldn't look him in the eye and still stand her ground. She'd felt betrayed by God but hoped it wouldn't put a breach in the relationship. It had. She knew it after she said it. Her face was pale and salty liquid flowed from her eyes. He could tell she needed him, but even more she needed faith in God. He would just let this slide and pray that it was all said in the heat of the moment. His hug seemed stiff to her and she could tell he was struggling to hold her close. He let her go and then walked to the desk to bring up a new topic or one less disheartening.

Bringing out the tiny black tape, he laid it in on the desk. "Here, you can have this."

Melanie was caught by surprise at the change of tone. "What is this?"

"Mark gave me this today. Do you want to know what is on it?"

"I doubt it, but play it, anyway."

He slid the tape in his answering machine. Together they held their breath waiting to hear. She was not sure what to expect but knew, by the way that Jason acted it would hit her hard. Suddenly the voice uttered and it was all too familiar: The icy metallic sound, the hate, the perversion, the evil that set the overtone for her continuing fear.

As the tape ended and the last message played, Melanie grew angry. The fear turned into a madness that made her sure she was going to make him pay. She was ready to do anything. It wouldn't be hard to put someone that sick in prison. She sure wouldn't feel guilty about having the future of someone like that in her hands. She abruptly turned and stood at the door. "Well, let's go. I'm ready to do the line up."

Jason was apprehensive at her confidence and demeanor that had changed so drastically between the time the tape started and ended. He smiled with a bit of question and tried to make her know he was with her, wholeheartedly. "Yes, you can do this. We'll be fine. *You* will be, I mean."

She wondered about the last statement as they made a steady pace to the car. Did he mean that *she* would be okay or was he indicating his concern of their future?

Chapter 12

Abby sat on the edge of the bed. The room was large and airy with flowing sheer drapes on French doors that allowed the sunlight in from the deck. The room made such a peaceful feeling and Abby loved being in there for that reason. It was her oasis. She found it to be the only place in the house that allowed her to let go of any problem and know that God was truly in charge of every circumstance. Her strength came from her Lord and she felt as if the bedroom was decorated the way Heaven would look.

For some reason, though the problems between Glenn and Abby had been overlooked by the recent events, there still stood a breach in their communication. To say it truthfully, they still had questions for each other; questions that needed to become freely asked and answered. Abby said a quick prayer to God for wisdom and guidance. She prayed for the right words. Rapidly the door to the bathroom opened and Glenn walked out with his towel around his shoulders and a pair of flannel pajama pants. He wiped the water out of his ears and smiled at Abby with a questionable look. Since he had missed a few days at the office, he was attempting to make up time on the weekend. Picking up the toothpaste, he lifted it up and waved it in the air as he finally broke the silence that had so long played its part in their marriage.

"I know it's hard to understand what is happening to us. I don't quite understand it myself. I feel like my work loves me more than you do. It's absurd to say but I feel that way."

Abby lifted her chin to show some manifestation of courage while deep inside she was so very timid and afraid. She said nothing for fear of what she *would* say.

"You don't have anything to say, Abby?"

"No Glenn, I have plenty to say. That's an absurd remark. You spend every waking moment at work and when you're here you're never mentally here. I can't try to make a marriage work by myself. You said you weren't having an affair with that woman, but why did you act like that's what was going on when I came to your office? Why did Carla see you with that woman? I want and deserve answers."

Glenn's eyes softened and he closed in on her space to sit close to her. She needed that at the moment. She was aware of the great efforts he was making. "I don't know why I led you to believe that. Maybe, it's nice to see you jealous. Maybe I wasn't thinking. Really, Ab, I wasn't. I'm sorry. You are my life, I've told you that before. If you weren't here, I would be lost. I need you. I need you to be my cheering section. I need you to be the mother to our children. No one could do it like you do. With all the stuff that's happening to our daughter, this family doesn't need to be torn apart by anything else. I can't stand the fact that you think you aren't necessary."

"Well, let's review what is happening here for a moment. Your mother thinks she can do it better. Glenn, I can't live this way anymore. It's not *just* her, though. It's you and I not sharing, communicating, loving."

His hand reached out to grab her a tissue. He always knew when she was about to cry. She loved that he knew her so well. Her eyes glistened in the shadow made from the window. She was always the brightest light in his life but the time that had passed between them seemed to have pulled them into an abyss. He knew she was just in her assessment of his mother and the living arrangements that had not been optional to her.

"I know it's hard having my mother live here. You two never got along. I know you've tried to make it work and I know at times she's an impossible woman. There I said it. I know it's true. She's overbearing and manipulative and condemning of everyone. But, for all that she is, she's also my mother and I felt like she needed to be with us when Dad died. His death was so sudden and I couldn't possibly let her stay in Nebraska by herself. Grace and David wouldn't let her move in with them. She never got along with David's wife either. I think it has something to do with her little boys being grown up. She's not easy, but then, we are not an easy family either. She doesn't relate to Mark at all. He doesn't seem to want to relate to anyone, much less my mom. I'm not sure *how* we can change things. She's fragile, she doesn't show it but she is. I think she's scared to be without Dad. He was there every time she woke up and every time she went to bed."

Abby spoke up with a tight but calm voice, "She's got to learn to live without him, Glenn. I'm tired of the battle. I can't do it with her anymore. She's hurting *us* and she's not helping with Melanie at all. Right now, our daughter needs our help and support and the only two things she could say when we brought her home were 'Life doesn't stop when tragedy strikes and you just have to plug on'."

Glenn laughed at her imitation of Barbara. "You do that too well." His upper lip curled up to the right in a sly smirk. She used to see him smile at her that way all the time. It was good to see it was coming back to him. His smile was warm and the ice that had been frozen so long was starting to thaw. His eyes shone like a star as the light peered in from behind the sheer flowing material that wisped from the open window. He loved her and he was bound and determined to fix what he'd help to break. The vase could be glued back.

"You know what I'm saying. That wasn't fair to Mel. She needs to feel like we are a haven and that she can have real feelings here. She's always been so strong willed and if she can't feel like she can express her pain with us, she could really have problems later. I don't want her to go to Jason every time she needs someone. You can help by showing Barbara she needs to find a place of her own and start her life without your father."

Glenn agreed as he stroked her soft ivory cheek. She loved the way it felt to have his hand touch her. He leaned over and kissed her softly on the lips. She was surprised but kissed him back. It was all coming back. He lifted his head up and pushed his fingers through her hair. "I'll talk to her about it." He stood up and went back to the sink to brush his teeth. Underneath a mouth of white foam he spoke into the mirror, "How about I look for a place for her and then I approach her? If she doesn't have to search for it herself she may be easier to convince."

Abby wasn't that cold of a person. "Not a great idea. She needs to have time to let it sink in. Tell her now and then both of you can find her a suitable place. I'll ease up on the tension between us and try to make things comfortable for her while she gets used to the idea."

"Thank you, Ab." He spit out the toothpaste and wiped his mouth. He was feeling better about the idea as the plans were verbally made. Turning around he walked into his closet and stared at the many tailor-made high designer suits he owned. The navy blue one stood out. He became oddly aware that lately he had been wearing gray and black more than any other color. Maybe the color change was a symbol of a meaningful change in his life. Of course it was a change. He grabbed it and found a crisp, white shirt to accent his dark features underneath the devastatingly beautiful coat and tie he would wear to his office. Even if it wasn't an official workday, he wanted to look professional.

Things were looking so bright to him and he questioned in his mind, *Why didn't we do this before? How did it get to this point? Whew, glad it's on it's way out of here.* He walked back out of the closet and before the smile could make its way into the mirror to his dear Abby, he noticed something.

Abby's eyes sparkled and her cheeks were blushed as he looked at her reflection. She had tears. He turned around suddenly. Before he could ask what he'd done, she spoke.

"Glenn, I'm so sorry."

"What in the world?"

"It's not easy to be your wife but I can't imagine not having you as my husband. All these things happening around us keep going through my mind. I can't stop the flood of thoughts and tears and fear. I'm so helpless sometimes and I just want you to be the one I talk to. I want you to be my source of compassion in this house. Will you forgive me for being so..."

He interrupted her and tilted his head in concern. "Yes! I forgive you and I do love you, Abby. You will never know how much. Will you forgive me too?"

She nodded as a shy grin came across her mouth. As he finished working on his tie they both noticed it sat a little crooked on his shirt. His smirk appeared again, he pointed to it and his forehead wrinkled with an unspoken plea for assistance. Abby's smile swelled as she stood up from the bed and walked over, placed her hands on the triangle of the tie and jimmied it around a bit till it was perfect.

Their eyes locked and the world disappeared. Time stood still and they moved closer. Simultaneously Glenn's head lowered and Abby's raised. Their lips touched and melted into one. It had been so long and yet it all seemed so natural as if the bad times had never occurred. Nothing outside of the room mattered. It was just the two of them. A marriage was reconciled. Abby knew it was only by her prayers that God's grace alone could bring them through the trials. Still, she was acutely aware that the trials may only have begun for the rest of the family.

Glenn looked at Abby and pursed his lips together. "I just love you. But can you believe it, I just brushed my teeth and now I'm hungry. Let's go eat something. Maybe Mom's still asleep." Laughter proceeded to fill the rooms and halls as they moved through the house in each other's arms.

Policemen wandered in and out of the station the entire time Melanie and Jason sat in the lobby waiting to do the line-up. She was nervous and her hands couldn't stop twisting and turning, much like her stomach was doing. She wanted to go to the restroom and throw up just to get it over with but the minute that she resolved to do just that, a lady behind the desk looked over and said that Officer Myers would be there in one minute to take her back.

Thoughts became muddled while she tried to come to the realization that she would be facing the one person in the world who could hurt her, even if it wasn't physical anymore. Her mind was messed up badly and she knew it would take a lot to recover from the fear that was lying so deep inside. The fear seemed at times to be anger and then intimidation. What else could she do but try to put the whole incident, as she would refer to it, behind bars and out of her conscience? If putting him in jail would make her feel better she was all for it. She really didn't believe that but saying it to herself over and over would surely sink in one day.

Would she remember anything when she stood facing him? Would she know his face? Would he look familiar? Then it hit her, she never saw his face. He had that horrifying mask on the entire time she had been awake. She wouldn't know him. She wouldn't be able to identify this monster. What would she tell them when she got in the room and saw no one? But she did hear him. She's heard him several times since then too, with his dreadful phone calls. His voice haunted her. She heard it in her sleep and she heard it when she was in the shower. She couldn't get away from it. She could identify him that way.

"Ms. Crawford. You ready?"

She looked up startled and a wave of nausea come upon her. Well, this was it. She had to tell herself, *Get up Melanie. You can and have to do this.*

Jason and Melanie stood at the same time, glanced at each other, locked hands and were escorted to a dark room. An attorney stood inside and put her hands on Melanie's back to lead her to a two-way mirror. She'd seen them several times on movies and television shows but it was different when it was for her use.

Inside the room stood the Prosecuting Attorney, Dave Mushane. She knew him from her father. "Melanie." He nodded his head in acknowledgment of her.

"Okay, bring them out," Officer Myers commanded.

Through a door on the other side of the mirror she watched as seven men walked out and formed a line. None of them looked familiar, but she knew they wouldn't. They all resembled each other very closely, with stern, sharp, angry features. Any one of them could have done it for all she knew.

"Melanie, look carefully and see if you recognize anyone. Take your time and just remember, they can't see you," Myers guided.

"You know, I never saw his face. He was wearing a mask the whole time." She bit her lip with angst and the hopes that this wouldn't mean she would be dismissed from identifying the monster.

The attorney closed her notebook and stood up, "I guess my client can leave. It would have been nice to know that little detail before we were dragged down here for this waste of time." She snapped a shot at Melanie.

"But, I do remember his voice." Melanie protested and suddenly looked quite astute, as well as irritated at the rudeness of the female attorney.

Jason grabbed her hand and held it tightly since she was obviously getting agitated.

Looking at Myers, "Can you have them do some sort of voice thing? Can she do that? He's called her and left messages. She remembers that. And I have the answering machine tape."

"Well, the tape will hold up more in court but we can have them say something that she remembers and if she can identify him then it *may* be admissible in court. Some judges don't like to rely on voice because it can be tricky and, although there are technological advances that can narrow it down, our state hasn't bought them. It's very expensive to become that high-tech." Myers wished he could say more that would be in her favor, but really the chances of picking out the same guy would be fairly impossible.

He turned to the attorney with the question in his eyes. She pursed her lips in resentment and then with a shrug of her shoulders, prepared to do a listening line-up. She didn't believe this was reliable either but she had to agree, for her client's sake of course. Her notebook was opened once more and her pen scribbled something down as she glanced at her watch. Apparently, this was not the most important item on her agenda.

"You have a lawyer, Ms. Crawford?" she asked, with a hint of irritation and belittlement.

"Yes, I have my father. He can represent me."

Stunned at the news, her jaw dropped in embarrassment, as she looked at her and smiled, "You're that Crawford? I had no idea it was Glenn Crawford's daughter. I apologize if this is hard on you. Also, for how nonchalant I have been towards you."

Nonchalant was lightly stating it, but Melanie accepted. "Thank you. Should I call him and have him here for this?"

"Doesn't he know you're here?" She was very surprised that Glenn was not there.

"No, he doesn't. He doesn't even know there is a case. I didn't tell him. I got the call and came down. He doesn't need to be bothered by this kind of thing. I can handle this end and he can handle the courtroom." Melanie was completely unaware of the protocol for a minor in a rape case and it showed, not just to the lawyer, but everyone else in the room.

Jason looked at her and wiped a bead of sweat falling close to his eye. It was stuffy in the little room, even with the lights off. His hands were damp and he was beginning to feel a bit nauseous. "Hey Melanie," he whispered, "I'm going to the restroom and I'll call your dad. I think he needs to be down here, just to make sure that you know what your rights are. I don't know about that lady, but I have a feeling she'll try to make you out to be stupid. She's trying really hard so far. I'll be right back." He kissed her on the cheek and the door opened, letting a flood of light and noise in. It was quickly shut and Melanie listened to the conversation between the officer and the attorney.

Noticing that she was being watched, the lady looked over and with the same tone of mockery she used before in her pathetic apology, she spoke. "Melanie, if your father is the lawyer in your case, he needs to be a part of every aspect. You need to let him know you're down here and he will be here immediately, I guarantee." A skillful smile crossed her lips, showing absolutely no respect for Melanie.

"Yes, you're right. Jason has gone to call my dad and he should arrive within the hour. Will that be okay with you, or do you have other pressing matters, such as a manicure or maybe you're late for the lecture 'How to Act Better Than Others'?"

She couldn't believe what had just come from her mind, much

less her mouth. It was so uncharacteristic for her to speak hatefully to anyone, other than her grandma. What was happening to her? She wondered why she was so angry. It wasn't all anger at people, but also at God. She felt betrayed and didn't know why, when she had been so careful about being the example that God would want, she would be hurt so badly. What was worse, her anger was tending to aim itself at the innocent people, Jason and this lady. She had to get a grip but deep down, the boiling in her stomach was becoming worse and harder to fight.

The lady looked at Officer Myers and pursed her lips with disdain and glared at Melanie. "You have a large mouth young lady. You had better watch the kinds of things you say. It might bite you in the trial later on. Mushane and Myers, I would think you could be better organized." She was embarrassed that a young girl could get the best of her, so she closed her little notebook, pushed her pen into her briefcase, closed it and stormed out of the room.

Chapter 13

Jason stood in the filthy police station public restroom. He wondered when was the last time it had been cleaned. His stomach was rolling, and his eyes were watering. There was nothing he could do but splash water on his face and hope that he would feel better. His hands were shaking and his knees were weak. He grasped the sink tightly with his left hand and turned on the faucet. The cool water ran over his fingers and it felt good to at least know that it was cold. He tossed water up onto his face as he hovered over the sink. It seemed to be better but then he looked up and the room was spinning. "What is wrong with you, Jason?" Not able to stand straight up, he wavered to the toilet and put the seat and lid down. As he sat down, his legs got more and more like Jell-o. His hands reached for the handicapped bars on the sides of the stall and he leveled himself with barely enough strength to hold on. He decided to rest his eyes for a moment and regain some strength. Time seemed to pass at a snail's pace and he wondered if Melanie was wondering where he went off to. He still hadn't called her father. He hadn't even made it out of the restroom. The door pushed open and he heard a pair of men's shoes on the hard grubby ceramic tiles. They went in the stall next to his and he sat, hoping not to draw attention to himself, since his stall door was wide open and he was just sitting on the pot lid. The noises were normal for the duration of the person's stay, however, he noticed that the man exited without even rinsing his hands. He made a mental note to grab a paper towel before handling the door knob, if he ever made it out of there.

His stomach started to feel less like he would lose his lunch and more like he would black out. He steadied himself and prayed that the feeling would go away. Just as he finished his call up to God to relieve him, his eyes rolled back, his hands slid from the handicapped rails, and his legs pulled out from under him. Though he was sitting down, he toppled to the left of the seat and hit his head on the wall, leaving a huge gash on his head and the blood began to poor freely. As the puddle became larger and more concentrated around Jason's limp body, he remained unconscious.

The door flew open once more and in walked a janitor. He strolled to the first stall and began to spray some cleaner and barely wipe the seat. He pulled the gray-watered mop out and swabbed with carelessness around the base of the toilet. It was obvious that he had no desire to do this job, though it was severely needed. He moved this same way, to the next three stalls and with very little concern, moved to the last stall. It was definitely a huge surprise to see a puddle of blood lying underneath a young man's face. He bent down and pushed on Jason's shoulder to wake him but there was no budge. He griped that another one of the bums was passed out in the bathroom, but this bum didn't look like the others he had seen. He figured that this was probably not a bum, due to the fact that Jason's clothes were pressed and neat, not to mention matching.

"Hey, we've got a problem in the men's room on the first floor. Can you send someone down who can patch up a large cut?… Yeah, I'll wait down here till you get here… Hey, Carl, can you grab me a soda on your way? Thanks." He put the walkie-talkie back in the cradle on the cart and tried to move around the blood to clean up the toilet around Jason.

It didn't even phase him that he was spraying a chemical around an injured person. He wiped down the toilet, better than the others, since someone official might see it. He didn't look forward to the mopping that he would have to do when the boy on he floor was picked up. Carl entered the bathroom and stood at the door.

"Where is the injured?" he asked.

"Here. I don't think he's a bum off the street. He looks like a student, if you ask me. Doesn't smell like beer. Maybe he got sick. You got a bandage?"

"Yeah, but it's gonna take more than a bandage. We're gonna need a gurney to get him out of here. Check his wallet and see if we can call someone."

The janitor leaned over, reached into the pocket he could see and pulled out a small brown leather wallet. It wasn't filled with very much money, but held a college ID, which confirmed his idea that this was a student.

They searched together through the wallet for more identification, but when they searched further, they noticed the vast amount of pictures that displayed the same person. She was beautiful.

"Man, she's gorgeous."

"Yeah, you ever been out with something that pretty?" Carl asked.

"Yeah, when my wife was younger, she was a pretty little thing. She's different now." He flipped through the pictures and they both giggled at their shallow and pathetic remarks, not remembering the real reason they were in the wallet to begin with. Suddenly the janitor jumped as his pants leg was tugged on.

"Help me get up." A weak, wispy sound emerged from the puddle of blood and Jason lifted his head slightly. He was confused but remembered that he blacked-out in the men's room.

"Sir, you gonna be alright?" Carl inquired.

"Where's Melanie?"

The two men looked at each other and winked. "Melanie," They said in unison with a dreamy tone.

"Who do you need us to get for you son?"

"Melanie. She's in the line-up."

"Is she in the line-up or is she identifying someone?" Asked the janitor.

"Identifying." His mouth was dry making it impossible to speak without a slur.

"Okay, well, you must have passed out. Do you think you can walk over to the sink and wash off? I'll go get your wife and Carl can hold on to you."

He nodded with very little strength as the two men lifted him from the floor. He was covered in blood and his head was throbbing. He thought he felt bad earlier but this was far worse than that. As they escorted him to the sink, he couldn't answer any of their multiple questions. They rattled on and on about something and he still had no ability to reason what they were really saying. The janitor left and went to the observation room, knocked on the door, and slightly opened it. He noticed a beautiful girl sitting in the folding chair and a policeman standing at the wall. "Ma'am, I'm sorry to bother you, but you're husband is in the men's room."

She was puzzled and said, "My husband? I don't have a husband."

"No? Are you Melanie? He asked for me to get Melanie."

"Yes." She jumped from her seat and terror struck her face. "Is he okay?"

They walked out into the hall and he tried to explain the little that he knew. She felt uncomfortable going in the bathroom but not enough to keep her in the hall away from Jason.

"Jason, Oh, my gosh. Are you hurt badly?" She ran to his side and wiped his head lightly with a bit of water. His eyes tried to focus on her but they began to roll back again. He got shaky and started to lose his stance.

The men and Melanie gripped him, holding him up. "Call 911. Did you already?" Melanie commanded. "Jason, tell me what happened. Can you hear me?"

His head wavered and his eyes opened as he tried to focus on her face. "Mel, I feel awful."

"Well, I guess so. You've busted your head open. Let's get you to the hospital and find out what happened." She looked at the men with eyes asking for assistance in carrying him out to his car.

The janitor asked her if he should still call 911 but she shook her head no and they all escorted him outside to the red sports car. Melanie grabbed the keys from his pocket and noticed that his wallet was not there. She became nervous and asked, "Where did his wallet go?" Her eyes shot a look at both of them and they looked at each other for the answer.

"Oh, goodness, ma'am. We got it out to find out who he was and I guess I left it in the bathroom. I'll be right back." He briskly left to go back inside and within seconds was back with the wallet. She didn't want to seem rude so she avoided checking it until she was away from the two men.

She got in, thanked them and sped away. Picking up Jason's cell phone, she dialed her father. It rang only once before she heard the usual, "Connor, Blake and Crawford."

"Sarah, this is Melanie, may I speak to my father please?" She sounded hurried so the conversation, which would normally last at least one minute, was cut short.

"Yes, Melanie. I'll put you through to him."

"Melanie? Sarah said you sound worried. You okay, honey?"

"Yeah, I'm fine but Jason fainted at the police station while I was doing a line-up ID and I'm heading for the hospital. Can you meet us there? And can you call his dad? I'm sure he'd want to know."

"What were you doing at the police station? You said a line-up? Mel, Are you serious? You did a line-up without telling me? Now, that's insane."

"Dad, you're right. You should have been there, I know, but can this be done another time? Just meet me in the emergency room. Can you do that, Daddy?"

"Sure, I'll be there in a few minutes. Be careful, Baby."

He hung up the phone and shook his head. He knew she was stubborn; much more like him than he wished. "Why didn't you tell me? Girl, you are, you are, so silly." He mumbled while he hurried to put his suit coat on. He pressed the button on the intercom, "Sarah, I'll be out of the office for a while. Please don't send any calls to me while I'm gone. Thank you."

"Yes, Mr. Crawford. Do you need me to call your wife and let her know anything?"

"Ummm, tell her to meet me at the emergency room and that it's *not* Melanie." He didn't want Abby to worry. She was so great at that. It was too much to expect. She would hardly be able to stay calm if the information was too vague. "Also, can you get me Marcus Lang on the phone? His work number should be there."

"Yes, I'll put him through when I get him on the line." Sarah was a reliable secretary. "Ok, here he is."

"Hey, Marcus, this is Glenn Crawford. How are you? Great. I

just thought you would want to know that Jason is being taken to the emergency room here, for passing out. If you'd like to take my number, I can be in touch with you."

Marcus was not very comfortable with Glenn, because he felt so inadequate as a father and man. He worked in a warehouse and he lost his wife to another man when Jason was just a young boy. She left with her older son from a different man and never returned. He never had much and worked very hard labor for the small amount he supported Jason with.

He extended his appreciation and explained that he was not able to leave work but would contact him on his next break. Glenn gave him the number and left for the hospital. He felt badly that Jason's father was so bound by work and wished that there was something that he could do that would allow Marcus to feel better about himself. Glenn could tell Marcus was uncomfortable so he excused himself off the phone and assured him that he would fill him in on what the goings-on were. Marcus apologized for not being able to leave and hoped Jason would understand.

"Grandma, Have you seen my red shirt? I left it on the top of the washer and now it's gone." Mark asked without a bit of accusation in his voice. Barbara got into character becoming abrasive.

"No, you should keep up with your things better." Her nose buried in a book, she never picked up her eyes to look him in the face. "What do you expect when you don't take care of your things?"

"You know, I wasn't accusing you of anything, but you are so defensive that you just assume that I'm coming at you that way. Are you insane, woman? Not everybody is out to hurt someone. It's been a while since you and I have gotten along. Yeah, come to think of it, we never did. I'm tired of you ragging on me, jumping down my throat, and mooching off the house. You are the most unpleasant woman I've ever tried to understand." With that, he noticed her eyes began to look up in his direction. "Oh, now what? You got something to yell at me about? Maybe so, but you know, Grandma, I may be stretching this a lot, but you and I could probably get along if you would give me a chance to show you that I'm not a horrible boy. I do have some redeeming qualities." He turned and walked to the doorway and stopped as he heard her clear her throat. He figured she would just lay into him, but she got simple and quiet.

"Mark, I'm not easy to get along with and I don't relate well with young people. Can you understand that?"

That remark was so out of character for her. He was expecting the worst blast from her, but this, this was unusual. "Yeah, but give it a chance before you push yourself so far away that no one will care if you are around or not."

He turned and walked up to his room and wondered if he had said anything that cut her to the core. He hoped that something had. He knew he had said some horrible things to her in the past and he wouldn't even blame her for being stand-offish to him for that. However, something really needed to change. The tension that had built up over the past week, between everyone in the house, was going to either hurt the family or they would become stronger for it.

The school day was not as long as it usually seemed. Though nothing was fun about it, he didn't dread being there. He enjoyed the fact that he was out of the house. He welcomed the idea of being normal. All the tragedies that were happening just seemed to make him scream for normalcy. At school, there were no phone calls, no sisters to mend the hearts of, no grandmas to dodge, and no mothers and fathers who pretended to love each other, although that seemed to be changing for the better. It had to be normal again one day. What could he do to fix it? He couldn't even fathom. His bed beckoned to him and he laid down with his knees up in the air and arms pulled behind his head. His thoughts were reeling over the past events and what the future was holding.

God had never played a part in his life. It wasn't something he could rely on, because, who had proof that God even existed? The Bible was a book of fictional stories that, though great and elaborate, and even occasionally gory, were probably written by prolific Romans and Greeks. They were great storytellers. He reasoned it in his head and always came to the same conclusion. God didn't exist. However, this day, he wrestled with his mother's firm belief and even gave in to the idea that she might be on to something. What was it about God that made his mom so peaceful, even through a trial? The firm belief *he* had that God didn't exist seemed to be crumbling.

"God, if you exist, we could sure use some help. I know that you don't know me, but my mom is into you, so you may be able to figure out who I am. Heck, if you *really* created me, you probably know me anyway. But, hey, my family could be doing a lot better. Can you help us out of the situations we're in? My sister means everything to me and I'm afraid that there is more danger around the corner. Please keep an eye on her and don't let anything else happen to her. Well, if you heard this, do what you can." He never felt more at peace than he did at that moment. Something inside him made him realize that his prayer was real and that God did hear it. His eyes closed and sleep fell upon him. He was at rest.

Barbara's eyes watered as she daydreamed out the window in the den. She was difficult, always had been. She didn't know how to change. Even if she wanted to become friends with the rest of the family, the efforts she would have to take would make her vulnerable to rejection. One thing she did keep contained in her cold heart was her love for God. She raised Glenn to believe in God and to place his trust in Jesus Christ, but that was the extent of her living for the Lord. It was hidden to everyone else. It was also something that she truly admired in Abby. She looked at Abby and wished that Abby's openness about Christ would become as audible in her.

"Lord, you have me in your hands and you have seen my anger. You have seen my jealousy and my weakness. I present you my mouth and my heart and ask that you will cleanse me completely and mend my relationships. I will need patience, a calm tongue and a willing spirit. Please help me, Lord."

She had a desire to be needed and her attitude could change and would have to if there were to be any amends made. She cradled her cup of coffee in one hand and took sparing sips, to make it last longer. It was lukewarm and yet, it seemed warm enough to her amidst her heavy thinking. She never even noticed when the phone rang.

It rang and rang, at least five times then the answering machine came on. She finally jolted from her seat and picked up the receiver. "Hello, hold on, let me turn down that machine...Ok, yes...Glenn? Hi sweetie...The hospital? Is it Melanie...Oh, Jason...Yes, I'll wait here and you call me when you find out something...Bye, bye." She hung up puzzled and a little bit scared. Something was wrong. Something was destined to destroy this family. What was it? She put a pair of white earmuffs on her head and tried to rest her head as she lay on the couch. Her mind went in different directions and sleep wouldn't happen. Her walk to the bathroom cabinet wasn't long, but seemed laborious for her. She felt weak and her nerves were getting the best of her. As she reached for the brown prescription bottle and poured out two tiny white pills, she felt assured that she would be asleep quickly. Popping them back, she didn't use water, just her own saliva. She looked forward to a mid afternoon nap. Earmuffs went back on and she quickly assumed the position on the sofa and fell fast asleep.

Chapter 14

The familiarity of the hospital was definitely not welcome to the Crawfords. It was only recently they had been frequent visitors. Nurses floated around the halls and people came in with urgency and some just out of sheer boredom, hoping for someone to notice them. The white board on the wall had about twelve names and the reason they were there. None of the reasons seemed all that dire. Most were associated with a stomach bug that had been floating around the town. Jason's name stood out to Glenn. He looked at the room number and headed down the corridor. As he reached the room, he noticed a familiar voice. Abby had beat him there.

"Where did you come from to get here so quickly?" He wandered over to her side and laid a light peck on he cheek. Her smile was slight and pleased. Melanie noticed the change but remained quiet about it.

"Oh, I was at the market and Sarah called me. I came as soon as I could. He fainted and we are still waiting on the results to come back from the lab."

"Dad, I'm sorry I didn't tell you about the line-up. It was something that came up this morning and I didn't think before I went down there. I didn't even do it. I couldn't remember what he looked like. I did tell them I would remember the voice, so they are going to let me listen and try to identify him. I promise you that I will have you with me next time. Okay, Daddy?" Her eyes pleaded and he folded from his frustration with acceptance.

Jason's eyes began to flutter as he tried to open them. His strength was waning and he couldn't speak. They held their breath waiting for a noise. He muttered Melanie's name and then fell back into a sleep.

Melanie grabbed her dad's hand as the doctor walked in the room.

Anxiety gripped her in the stomach. "What is it? Why did Jason faint?"

"Are you Jason's father and mother?"

"No, his father works in a different town and his mother isn't around. He's our daughter's boyfriend but we will be responsible for him. What's wrong?"

"Well, it appears that he was poisoned with Rubidium."

"What? How? Did he breathe it or touch it?" Melanie demanded.

"No, it's uncommon for it to be found in the body any other way but ingested by food or drink. It's used in many Chemistry classrooms but not normally 'sold' in your local drugstore. Does he take any classes?" The doctor glanced up from his chart and looked at Melanie for answers. She was looking to him for answers.

"No, he's not taking any science classes this semester. He doesn't even go to the science building. I can't imagine any place he would have gotten something like that in his food. Is it a liquid or what?"

"Well, it's a common element that has no flavor and no odor, but can be very poisonous in large amounts. Small traces of it can be found in mineral water, or even tea and coffee. Also in tobacco. Does he smoke?" Everyone replied no. "He will need to sleep until his medication wears off. He's lucky there wasn't enough in him to kill him, but that would be rare." The doctor turned to leave and was caught by a remark.

Abby broke her silence and smiled, "He's blessed, not lucky. It isn't chance that's saving him. He has God on his side, Doctor." Melanie's eyes darted to the stark white, clean walls. She knew her mother was right but her heart was so broken and cold that she didn't want to listen to the truth. The doctor nodded with little appreciation. Apparently he figured *he* was the real reason that people would be ok. Abby let it slide and Glenn held her hand tightly.

Melanie was confused by the information. Was it poison or could it have come from the latte they had at the coffee shop? Considering all of the things that had gone on, the possibility of something sinister became a reality. She put it all in the back of her head and sat down next to the bed, waiting for Jason to awaken. It wasn't more than an hour or so that went by when his eyes opened and he smiled at the only face he wanted to wake up to. His smile turned to confusion as he wondered about his surroundings. They were not familiar and he was sure he didn't get there on his own will. It was stark white, bleach clean, and the sheets were crisp. He wasn't hooked up to anything but the bars on the twin hospital bed made him feel restricted. Melanie pressed the button on the side of the bed, which pushed the head of the mattress to move up. He felt better when she did so.

"What happened to me?"

"You passed out in the police station. The doctor said you had a poisonous substance called Rubindium?" She looked for help with the word.

"Rubidium." Glenn spoke up correcting her pronunciation. "How?"

"Well, he said it could've been from the coffee we went for this morning. It's found in teas and coffees. But I wonder why I didn't get sick, too? We had the same thing." Melanie began her suspicions again, but the rest of the family just brushed it aside as coincidence.

"You can get out soon. How do you feel, now?" Abby asked.

"Well, I can honesty say I feel better than I did. My head hurts like crazy."

"You bumped your head on the bathroom wall. Some janitors found you. There was blood all over the floor and you couldn't wake up. I was so scared."

"Well, I think I'll be fine. I am tired. Can you see about getting me something for this headache?"

The nurse answered the intercom with much speed and soon came in with a great pain reducer. It put Jason to sleep in minutes. Melanie and Abby sat with him, while Glenn excused himself back to the office.

"Sweetheart, I will be home around five or so." He kissed Abby's cheek and Melanie stood stunned, but excited at the odd site of her parents' personal display of affection.

He left Melanie with many questions for her mother. Since it was

Saturday, and there was nothing pressing on the schedule, they began to discuss the new relationship between Abby and Glenn. It was a great day, despite the surroundings. In the occasional awakenings that Jason had, the conversation was the introduction of a brand new friendship between Melanie and her mother. They shared thoughts and feelings that were so intimate, so personal. They shared laughs, cries and it was as if there had been no relationship between them before that day. Abby was sensitive to the fact that Melanie was still uncomfortable with talk of the rape but she began to inquire about it, even so.

"Melanie, I know this has been difficult for you but I just wanted to let you know, you can tell me anything."

"Mom, I really am fine about the rape." She was lying as she gazed out the window trying to make light of the issue. "I guess I'm just stronger than everyone thought. I don't dwell on it so I don't feel like it can hurt me anymore."

"Well, honey if that's true, then I am glad God has brought you out of it, but if you're trying to hide it, then it will definitely haunt you. Why would you go to the police station and do a line-up if you didn't want to be reminded of it?"

The probing started to wear on Melanie and she was getting restless, but knew her mother knew her best. "Mom, I know it's hard to understand, but I thought that would help me put it behind me. I will be honest, I know I try to act like I'm not bothered, but I see it when I close my eyes. Over and over. I say I'm fine but I'm not. I keep thinking that whenever I'm alone, wherever it is, he can see me and that when I'm out in public, he can see me and that if I'm asleep in my own bed, he is outside my window, watching me. It's not right to be so scared and I figured that I could get some relief by knowing that the guy was in prison."

"You're right. Knowing that would be a relief. But, I don't know that you are coming to terms that your life will never be the same. You may have the joy of knowing that he is gone, but the memories, sweetheart, those don't go away."

"Mom, you don't honestly believe that there is not a day that will come when I don't see the mask or feel the pain. I believe that it will come. I believe that with all my heart."

"God can do anything to you, but it won't be gone in a flash. I know. Melanie, I understand you."

"You know, God can do anything, but He didn't. He didn't help me at all. I prayed, I screamed and I cried but it still happened. It doesn't matter what God *can* do, but what He didn't do, Mom. And no, you can't say you understand. I'm not sure you or anyone ever will. I appreciate you thinking you can, though."

Abby looked at her and tears filled her eyes. The conversation was bound to end up here, she thought. She stood up and turned toward the window, looking out into a beautiful sunny sky with no cloud in sight.

"Mom, what's the matter?"

Abby never turned back around and she began a long story that turned her heart inside out. She'd never shared it before, with anyone.

"Melanie, I was in the seventh grade. I had a short walk to school and then after school I would go home with a friend and stay at her house. It was fun and I had a great time. That friend had a brother who was seventeen years old and he wasn't there very often. He played football at the high school and usually didn't have anything to do with Jane and me. We were just two kids to him. It was really rainy outside that day and the two of us had to play inside her house and there was some other friend over with her brother. It seemed like the house was so large and that we wouldn't be in their way, but I managed to find myself in the large pantry. Her mother was in the barn doing something and I honestly don't know where Jane was. Her brother came in and said he was getting some apples for himself and his friend. I don't know where the friend was either. He started making small talk and it seemed really wonderful that this older, handsome boy was talking to me, a lowly seventh grader. I guess it wasn't all that long of a time he was in there with me, but I remember that the time seemed to stop. He asked me what school was like and started moving closer. He handed me a round, fragrant, green apple and bit into his own. His hand stroked my hair and he said I was beautiful. I didn't think anything about it. I was flattered. He threw his apple into the wastebasket, though he'd only taken three bites out of it. It's funny the things you do remember. He grabbed my hand and held it in his and then put his other hand behind my neck. He pulled me close to him and tried to kiss me. I didn't resist because I didn't understand. I don't know what was going through my head but then he pulled on my clothes and before I knew it, he had me on the ground. I cried and he told me that I was in trouble if I made any noise or told anyone. He got up and left after he was finished and I sat there with no idea how to get up and leave. I never told anyone. My mom never knew and I haven't told your father either. I know what you feel. And yes, God can do anything. He can help you bury the hurt and the pain, but you will be haunted by the scene, forever. It just won't be as bad. Honey, let God heal you. Open your heart and don't close him off. He is your only cradle. I can't even do that for you, even though I want to so badly."

"Mom, I don't know what to say. I'm sorry. You do understand."

They held each other tightly and both began to realize that the common bond would bring them so close they would never be the same. Melanie had a best friend in her mother. She felt so comforted, yet she hurt for her mother. How could she keep that secret so long?

For the first time in days, he went into the science room. His hand stroked the long black lab table and he caressed the Bunsen burners as he walked down towards the cabinet of vials that held many gases, metals, semi-metals, and liquids. He knew his way around the room and he knew how to create anything. The mask he created was nothing. That was just the basic plastic made from a mold. He had the power at his hands and he knew how to use it. It wasn't going to be hard to make the world revolve around his wishes. All he had to do was create the next incident from the collection of concoctions in this particular chemistry room.

"Good-morning, Stan." A man with wide-rimmed glasses and a lab coat passed him and stooped down reaching to unlock a locked drawer. Papers and file folders were in order as he rummaged through looking for the correct file. "I guess I left some information on this week's lab. The test is coming. I know you are probably ready, but you need to practice your formulas. They'll be tough." He stood and smiled.

"Doctor Monroe, I have a few theories I'd like to test out. Perhaps I could use the lab tonight after classes are over. Would you mind if I stayed? It shouldn't take too long."

"I don't think that will be a problem, Stan. I know I can trust you to be careful. Just remember that whatever you get out, you put away and clean up after yourself." Doctor Monroe put his files back into the drawer and stood straight up. "You say you have some theories? I'd like to hear them. But, you know that won't change the answers on the test." He smiled large and toothy as his glasses were raised by his round cheeks. He was known to laugh at his own quips, but Stan was not going to miss his chance to schmooze the teacher.

"Oh, I'm probably wrong about all the ideas I have. Your test will definitely be quite a challenge but I know I won't be able to change anything that is scientifically proven, especially in your lab." They exchanged a smile and both went to their own tasks, while students carrying enormous duffel bags filed in and sat at empty spaces on the lab table.

Thoughts were only of the next plot. Stan had tricks up his sleeve and he was planning on using every one of them. He knew that Melanie was doing a line-up, and he grinned at the idea that someone would take the fall for him and then terror could take up again. He had some time to figure out his next move, and he grew excited at the fact that he would be forced to remain silent for a little while. His nose and ears turned read with urgency when he began to think of the amount of time that it would take before he could actually turn on her again. She must think that he is behind bars. He hoped that somehow, someone would be chosen in the line-up. Someone had to. His plan would go bad if she couldn't identify someone other than him.

The Saturday study session began and the gas burners worked well, emitting the burnt chemical smell and heating up beakers with various colored liquids and gasses. It was a pungent room with varying intellects. The semester tests were around the corner and panic was upon most people in the room. Some students studied Chemistry for fun while others in the class were just fulfilling a requirement. Stan was in love with the study. It meant he was in charge of the elements that were around him. He could change things whenever he pleased, with one chemical or another. He loved the power.

Chapter 15

Glenn had a way of making people do things for him. Monday was a totally wild day around the police station but everyone scurried around getting the line-up ready for Glenn and Melanie. Being the attorney of choice in the city, Glenn had a powerful voice and people moved quickly. The line-up took about twenty minutes to gather up.

Melanie tried to remember what the rapist had said to her. Her mind walked through the entire scene and her heart began to beat harder as she searched her memory for a sentence. *"You're a phony, a fake."* He said it over and over and she couldn't shake the tone of his voice. He hated her and she never knew who he was or is.

"Well, Ms. Crawford. Can you give us a statement that you particularly remember him saying to you?" The officer in the observation room was very kind and gave her some ease as he mentioned that she only need to listen to the men say the phrase and pick out one that she was sure sounded like him.

It was easy. There was nothing to it. She trained herself to believe it and said, "He kept saying, 'You're a phony, a fake'." Glenn's hand held her shoulder as he stood above her. He was protective of her and the other police and staff made a point of being overly kind to both of them.

The door opened and in walked the same lady defense attorney as the last time. Melanie's eyes rolled and she made it known she wasn't happy to see this woman. The lady looked at her and gave a stiff smile, then held her hand out to Glenn, "Glenn, good to see you." She glanced at Dave Mushane with disdain.

"Margaret, you too. You've met my daughter, I see."

"Yes, at the last line-up. We…met." She turned her back and looked to the officer, "Let's get this show on the road, shall we?"

A button was pushed. "Let them out." Rugged men walked from

one side of the wall to the other and stood in front of black lines that showed their approximate height. "Gentlemen, when we call your name, please step to the black line and speak into the speaker. You are to repeat this line, 'You're a phony, a fake.' Just state it clearly and step back."

"Number one, you're up," the officer charged.

His voice was grainy and deeper than she remembered.

"Number two."

His voice was higher.

The next three were obviously not it but then number six came forward. Something was eerie about it and she began to hear the voice clearly in her head. "I need him to say it again." She requested and everyone in the room looked at her, with fear and astonishment. She had the feeling that none of them believed that this would work.

"Again, please number six."

"You're a phony, a fake," he said. He said it with less enthusiasm this time. He had a vague realization that he might have said it the wrong, yet right way.

"Okay, thank you. Number seven."

Not him, but number six... She couldn't get him out of her mind and she blurted out, "It's him. Number six. I think it's him."

"You think?" Margaret questioned her with disdain and Glenn picked up on it. Turning to Melanie and making a harsh glance at Margaret, Glenn asked her, "Honey, are you sure? Is that him?"

"Yes, he said it the same. It sounded like him." She really wasn't positive but it was somewhat a relief to have and idea that possibly he was in jail. But what if it wasn't him? She didn't even want to think of that possibility. It had to be him. The voice sounded so familiar and she didn't want to think that he was still able to hurt her.

"Take him away. Thank you, Ms. Crawford. We know that was difficult for you," the officer said and walked out.

"We'll be in touch. You realize, Glenn that this kind of ID isn't going to hold up very well in a courtroom." Margaret tried to hide the fact that she was a rude woman, but it didn't help.

"Margaret, you know, we'll see what the jury thinks about the tape that we have also. Maybe you have a swinging chance, but it's not over before it begins." He escorted Melanie out and into the parking lot.

"Do you think it will be okay, Daddy?"

"Margaret sounds intimidating, but she didn't graduate with the best scores. She skated through and just happened to have a cousin in the pool. He got her a job as a defender. She was assigned. Don't worry, I'm a great attorney and I can stand up to her in a courtroom. The jury will love you and be ready to throw the shackles at this guy. I can't believe I don't want to attack him. I figured that I would jump on him the minute I saw him, but now, I just want justice."

Melanie got into the car and they drove in silence, absorbing the events.

TWO MONTHS LATER

The courthouse was beautiful, with regal columns made of hard mahogany wood. Large rooms off the atrium were the backdrop of many convictions or dismissals. Pay phones hung in a row on the left side of the wall. The bathrooms were marked by arrows down separate corridors. Offices with well-known justices' names were lining the right hand side of the wall. The atrium had a large circular iron rail, which spiraled up to the second floor. Eyes were instinctively drawn to the beautiful stained-glass skylight that took its place as the entire ceiling. People flooded up and down at a hurried pace and those who were there routinely didn't give the place a second thought. No one seemed to notice its intricacies: the details on the wood, the marble, gigantic, round windows and the magnificent staircase. No one had time or the longing to observe the surroundings. Lawyers did their lawyer things. Judges walked from one chamber to the next. Convicts in orange were ushered in and out held by police officers on each side. Family members were neither happy nor sad by any outcomes. In most scenarios, it wasn't the type of setting for glorious reunions.

Glenn fit in well. He was comfortable since this was his element.

It was tough, sometimes brutal and terribly high-powered. He lived to make others pay for their wrongs. He loved his job and he loved the strength. He *was* the whole package when he wore his suits and carried his black leather briefcase. He had secrets in there. The defendants were in his complete control. He could make or break a case just by using the information he had.

The case would begin shortly. Each attorney got a chance to decide which jurors would serve them best. People who had received special notification for jury duty were told where to go and what to do. They all looked so discontented to be there. As thirty-some odd men and women were shown to their seats, the defense attorneys sat at a desk with pens and legal pads. Glenn and another lawyer from his firm sat at the opposite desk with the same supplies. Glenn and Margaret exchanged hard eyes. Margaret thought she was tough in the courtroom, until that day. Her confidence was diminished by the fact that Glenn sat opposing her. How could she possibly win a case like this? His passion would be strong and his words would be tough. She figured she'd already lost but would give it her best shot, anyway. It was her job. She had been assigned to defend the monster.

The questions for the jurors were generic and never focused directly on the actual defendant. "Have you or anyone you know, ever been a victim of sexual crimes?" "Are you able to give a verdict of guilty based on the testimonies of the witnesses?" "Do you think you will be able to give a fair sentence, even if that means the harshest punishment available?"

One by one, people were dismissed if either attorney decided they wouldn't help their case. It finally came down to twelve jurors who were willing to give generic answers and keep in any opinion they may have. Jury selection was complete. The trial would begin approximately one week later.

Glenn was pleased with the representatives on the jury. He felt that they were probably sensitive to this type of case and would handle it well. He could read people very well, which was one reason he was revered in the courtroom. His plan worked well most of the time. He was very familiar with every judge. He knew how to get on their good side. The jury members usually found him to be straightforward, concise and very thorough. He looked especially forward to this case. The justice he would see would be enough to put his heart and mind at ease. Melanie didn't deserve what happened to her. He was anxious to see that her rapist would pay heavily. He would be ready with everything he could throw at the defense.

It may be paying off for me to follow you, Mr. Glenn Crawford, Stan thought to himself. Just knowing small details about the case against someone else made his heart race and his mouth salivate. It was as if he'd just bitten into one perfect steak.

He stood at the door of the courthouse and one by one people came out of the chambers where he had seen Glenn enter. After an hour or so those chosen to sit on the jury exited and mingled a little bit in the atrium. He picked out one, that's all he would need. The man was about his size, his same hair color. The rest of the details could be easily duplicated. He was sure he could come up with one spectacular mask that would certainly deceive anyone.

He sauntered up to the man and looked at him as they both leaned over to take a drink from the water fountains on the wall. As they finished, Stan wiped his hand on his mouth, and said, "Boy, I guess today isn't my day. I sure hope yours is better."

"It's not too bad. I hope you start having a better day." The man was nonchalant and had no desire to be bothered, but Stan had to make it work. It was too important.

"If I could get the car started I could certainly make it to my appointment. I can't believe my wife didn't come pick me up after I phoned her that the car was having problems."

"You should call Roadside Assistance." The man began to walk away, unconcerned. Then he turned and decided that he was not going to be that cruel, to anyone.

"Where do you need to go? I might be able to give you a lift," he said.

Everything was looking better as Stan's eyes lifted up and he grinned a toothy grin. "Are you sure that's not a problem? I need to get to Wilson Lumber Warehouse. I'm the assistant manager. Man, I'd sure appreciate it." They walked to the white, mid-size vehicle in the parking lot and both got in. Small talk continued for a while.

"So, do you know how to get there? You're just driving and didn't ask me any questions," Stan said.

"No, I don't guess I do. I was just going the direction of my office. I'm sorry. Just tell me where to go. I can't believe I was doing that. This whole court thing is making me a bit weary. I don't want to sit and listen to any lawyers. I don't really care anything about the case, and frankly, I have better things I could do with my time. You know what I'm saying?"

Stan took offense to that remark. What did he mean he didn't care anything about the case? This was *the* case. And how dare he demean his precious Melanie. She was worth the trial. Just to see her face would make it all worth it.

He shrugged it off and started giving directions. After about thirty minutes of driving, the man began to wonder if they would ever get there.

"Are we close? I didn't expect it to be this far out."

"It's not."

"Where are we going?" he demanded as he slammed on the brakes and served onto the side of the road. Noticing that there had been no other cars on the road for some time began to unnerve him and he reached for his cell phone in his pocket. Stan quickly pulled a knife out and knocked the cell phone out of his hand with a swipe of the blade.

"Get out," Stan said, extremely calmly and without even one blink of trepidation. He waved the knife in the man's face.

The blade was enough to coerce him as he scooted across the console and gearshift, out the passenger door toward Stan. His face was full of horror and he began to beg for some answers.

"If you want my car or my money, fine, take it." He went for his wallet and Stan laughed at him, while, at the same time scraping the sharp metal across the man's knuckles. They were raw and bleeding profusely. The man stared in awe at the damage done to his hand and realized that there would possibly be more to come.

"I'll get your wallet after I kill you. I think that might be the easiest way to do this. I can't have you reversing my weapon on me, now can I?" He thrust his left arm and grabbed the man's shirt pushing him to the ground face first. "Don't look up, it will be worse." The sheath of steel penetrated deep as it hit bone and muscle. The man's back arched upward and then his arms, which held him up, gave way and he lay prone on the ground.

Stan wriggled the wallet out of the pocket and opened it up, staring straight at the face of the man he'd just casually killed. Evan Garrison Jurney. Stan read the name out loud, rolled his eyes, and then continued to read the specifics. "Birthdate, 4/12/78, huh. He's older than I thought. Oh well, that's not a big deal. 224 Bridgestone Cove. Must be middle-class. I can fill his shoes perfectly. Besides, I do believe they are going to be my size." He smiled.

"Well, Evan, I guess I have to put you to work. You've got a long night ahead of you." He spoke to the dead man as if he were alive. Bending down, he put his arms under Mr. Evan Jurney's and pulled him over gravel and grass. He shoved him like a bag of potatoes into the backseat, carelessly bent his legs to make them fit and slammed the door. As he got into the driver's seat, his head began to fire up, thinking of the plans for the evening. He had a large job to do. He was relieved that the professor had allowed him to use the lab after hours. Without the extra time in the lab, he wouldn't have been able to create his mixture that would establish his next plot.

Margaret demanded tasks be done from the moment she entered her office. Everyone in her office dreaded her presence. She was rude and abrasive, not to mention very pushy. Her ways were best and she expected most things to be done yesterday.

"Gail, you are going to have to run me a list of all of Gabe Shaw's priors. I need it quickly. I have to see what we are dealing with."

"I did that weeks ago, Ms. Young. I put it in your box."

"Now, don't you think I'd have it in my hand if you'd done that?" she snapped.

"Yes, I'll go run it. Again." Gail didn't feel like putting up with her boss, but she had to support herself somehow. She was studying law herself and would someday be the one giving orders. She also knew that when that day came, she wouldn't be like Margaret.

"Gail, when you get it I want you to come in my office and we'll discuss Gabe's defense. Ms. Crawford's past history may need to be an issue we can use to distract the jury. The only thing we can do is make it look like she asked for it." Although deep in her heart, she knew it wasn't right nor was it possible to make Melanie look like a bad girl.

"That's sick. Rape isn't something a person asks for."

"Whose side are you on? Help me win this. If I can beat Glenn Crawford, do you know what that will do for me?" She turned toward her phone and motioned carelessly for Gail to leave.

Gail was glad to exit the room. She couldn't care less if Margaret got ahead in the business. She also didn't care if Gabe Shaw got put in prison for life. That would be just one less rapist.

Chapter 16

Glenn approached his mother with sensitivity and a touch of fear. He didn't like to upset her and he didn't want to take sides. He prayed to himself, "God, I haven't visited you lately, but I think now would be a great time to start. Mom may not understand what I'm about to say. Please help me say the right things and give me the words of comfort that she'll need. Thanks."

"Mom, can I talk to you? This is something I should have done a couple of months ago, but then everything got a little busy around here. Abby and I have discussed it and I think it would be good for all of us if we looked for an apartment for you."

"Glenn? You don't want me here? Or wait, Abby doesn't want me here!"

Her defensive attack began to grow loud, as she started accusing Abby of everything under the sun. He allowed her the opportunity to clear her mind.

"Mom, it isn't anything like that. We know that you aren't adjusting to our family so well and I would like to make it easier on you. You could use a place of your own and it's just that simple. It's not that you can't come over. You can. In fact, we would like to find you a place close by. I will pay the rent and the utilities. Abby wouldn't mind if you were to join us for dinner every now and then. It's just that since you moved in, my relationship with Abby and the kids has been strained. I tried to make you feel so at home, I neglected them."

His eyes searched her for some semblance of understanding, but there was only anger.

"That's just how I expected to be treated here, but not by you. I can't believe that *you* want me out? I took care of you all your life and I guess you have decided that I'm too much to take care of. Fine, and Glenn, ease your mind. I don't need help finding a place. I am perfectly capable." She stormed out of the room and her feet pounded down the hardwood floor.

"Well, that could have gone better." He sat down on the barstool and cleaned an apple on his shirt, and prayed. "Thank you God. I know it could have been better, but it's Mom. I understand that."

Abby pulled up in the driveway so he stood to go out and meet her halfway. She smiled, surprised, as she looked up and saw him walking toward her. It wasn't everyday that he was greeting her at the door.

"Hey sweetheart. How did the jury selection go?" She kissed him on the cheek and he smiled gently at her.

"It went fine. I think we've got a major road ahead of us, but I do feel good about it. Look, I *just* talked to Mom. I know we decided to do it earlier, but…"

"Believe me, I understand. That's fine. How is she?" She was genuinely concerned.

"Not great. She said she doesn't need my help finding a new home. I'll give her some time to get herself together, but I think she'll be fine."

"Glenn, I'm sure she's not mad at you. But I can see where she would be hurt. I'll take the blame if you need me to."

"No! You've taken enough. It's fine, Ab. It's going to work out." They walked into the kitchen together, and Glenn broke the quietness.

"You know what I did?"

"What?" Her face showed true enjoyment in the recent changes made in their relationship. Hope won out and God's grace poured out onto them, bringing a peace they had forgotten they once owned.

"I prayed. Really and honestly talked to God." His smile showed his joy, along with a sense of astonishment.

They had discussed prayer often and how important it was. Glenn had never been fond of the idea. It seemed more like a waste of time; talking to something that he couldn't see. However, through the years of marriage, Abby had been faithful to pray in every situation and it gave her such peace. Sometimes things didn't go the way she would have chosen, but it always turned out fine. He wondered if that was what "God's Will" was.

"Glenn? Are you sick?" she joked as she put her palm against his forehead. "You don't have fever. What made you do that?"

"Ha, ha. I figured that when I was telling Mom I would need some help. I have huge cases and I don't need assistance, but Mom is different. I actually felt a lot better about it. Peace? Is that what that is?" His hand ran over over her cheek and he lightly pinched her dimple.

"Yes. It feels good to have God on your side. You know, we *could* pray *together.*"

He stopped her, "Not so fast. I'm just not used to it yet. It may take me some time."

Her face dropped in disappointment, but she was proud of his baby steps. She would be an encouragement and not push. He was terrible at pulling away. She knew where to draw the line.

"Sweetie, where's Melanie? Do you know if she's home?" she asked.

"I have no idea. I don't imagine so."

"So, you think the jury will be fair?"

"I think the jury will be able to see this man for a rapist and put him away. I know that the prosecutor will be able to show very little physical evidence, but Melanie identified his voice. When she gets on the stand..." He was interrupted.

"She's getting on the stand? Glenn, why? Do you know what you're asking her to do?"

"What else could make a jury know how horrible he is?"

"They have the answering machine tape for that." She became angry.

"I don't think she's going to have a problem with it, Abby. She's been strong through the whole thing."

"No, she hasn't. It's all an act, can't you tell? She and I have talked. When Jason was in the hospital, we discussed some things; very serious and complicated feelings. These things don't just go away. Trust me, she's not ready."

"What are you talking about?"

"Glenn, a woman has a mind that is capable of replaying something over and over, without anyone knowing it. Believe me, I know." She looked at the ground and then focused her eyes in his.

"Abby?"

"I guess now is a good time to open this can of worms." She sat down at the breakfast table and began to pour her heart out. His face fell into his hands as he cried. He grabbed her and hugged her hard.

"I'm sorry I didn't tell you. I feel horrible for keeping something like this away from you for so long, but I never thought I would need to tell that story. I never thought my daughter and I would have this in common."

"It's all right, Abby. I'll take it easy." The embrace lasted for an eternity until the back door opened and Jason walked in with Melanie.

"Hey, you guys. Are we interrupting?" He chuckled, uncomfortably.

"Mom, are you okay? Your eyes, you've been crying?"

"I am fine, Melanie. I just needed to share something with your father." Her eyes told Melanie what they had been discussing.

"Oh, well, we can leave."

"No, baby. I'll fix us some supper and we can sit in here and eat like a family, if Mark ever gets here." Abby rose gracefully, as usual. Her appearance was lovely in the beautiful light of the pale yellow and blue kitchen.

"Where's Grandma?"

"She's busy thinking." Glenn spoke up quickly, looking at Abby with a small smile.

"Buck, do you believe in God?"

"Well, I certainly don't think the explosion thing is true. I kind of think there may be something that made all of this." His hands motioned around.

"My mom's a Christian. She prays, goes to church and stuff. Weird, huh?" Mark replied.

"There's nothing weird about that. She's got a focus," Buck said, trying to sound intelligent. "You don't think there's a God?"

"Well, I'm beginning to think that maybe there's someone. My mom isn't dumb, so I don't think she'd fall for something off the wall. She wouldn't go with a group to meet a spaceship or commit a mass suicide. She's just kind of…good. You know what I mean?"

"You think that's all it takes? Being good I mean? So you want to believe in someone?" Buck asked.

"I don't know. I guess so. It would be nice to have a focus. I guess I would believe if I saw proof or could reason it out in my head."

"Yeah, but I think that's what faith is; knowing something even if you can't see it. I would say you are well on your way to a focus, compadre."

They both laughed. "I need to go. I've got some work I got to get done before I get grounded. I'll see you in the morning." Mark headed home and walked into a rare but genuine family dinner.

Chapter 17

When the car reached its destination, Stan got out, popped his neck and stretched his arms. He left the car in the parking lot of the apartment complex. It was only about a minute before he returned with a box filled with strange paraphernalia. He pushed the box into the passenger seat and with the keys in the ignition he left skid marks on the pavement. He ended up in a remote country area just outside the town.

Evan was heavier than Stan imagined. He struggled to turn him over since the corpse lay distorted in the back seat of his own car. Stan managed to work the upper body over allowing Evan to face upwards. He grabbed a bottle containing a thick liquid. He poured it gently and deliberately over the face of the man whose identity he would soon take over. It flowed slowly into each crevice of his facial features. It was quick to dry. Time was of the essence. Stan looked carefully at the mixture and back at his watch. When it was completely dry, his hands gingerly gripped one side of the mask and pulled lightly. It came off in one piece. Stan was grateful that it didn't tear. That would have just prolonged his next project. All he had to do now was leave the body of one unidentified man in a secluded area.

He pulled the body out of the car and left, without a second look. He drove to the highway near his apartment complex and pulled to the shoulder. He grabbed a bottle of disinfecting cleaner and a white cotton cloth. Spraying and rubbing any and all areas of the car that might have a fingerprint on it, he was carefully covering his tracks. It was beginning to turn very dark and the moon was in a quarter waning phase. The light was minimal but perfect to make him invisible to drivers on the highway. When the cleaning was done to his standards, Stan slowly opened the car door with the rag. He slid out in a hunched position, grabbed his box, wiped the door handle on the outside and ran down the embankment clutching his new face to his chest. He made it!

His apartment was dark and mysterious. Furniture was sparse to say the least. The couch was more of a yard lounge chair. There was no television, no radio. The fridge and stove were avocado green, which matched the hard, stained carpet covering the floor. He waltzed directly to his bedroom, which was nothing more than a mattress on the floor, with a crumpled sheet across it. He opened the closet. The large walk-in closet was another story. What better place to keep secrets than a closet. No one would think anything would be in there, since the living space was bare.

He carefully set the box on the floor. His hand reached inside for the newly created mask. He'd made masks before. He'd made two, to be exact. They weren't hard to create. It seemed so basic to him. He'd always had a love for science and this was the best way he knew to use his vast knowledge. He trimmed the part of the mask that hung off the hairline. He didn't need the mask in his hair. As he stretched it over his face, the image in the mirror was horrific. He loved it.

The eyes were still covered. He pulled it off and began to trace out the form of the eyelids with a sharp dissection knife. He worked meticulously on the opening of the mouth, nose and ears. It took some time to do. He was so precise that when he put it on the second time, there was no way to tell that the new Mr. Evan Garrison Jurney was a mask. He removed it once more and draped it on a hook in the back of the closet. His thoughts wandered to his clothing choices. Would Evan be caught in the shabby clothes that Stan wore? He knew he would need to make a special trip and splurge for some business suits, on Evan's pay of course. He wondered again if Evan had a family. Would someone miss him? Was he single? It didn't really matter. He never thought to check for a wedding ring, but he didn't remember seeing one either.

He took a seat at his cluttered desk in the closet. He pulled out the wallet, which held several one-dollar bills and a five. "He didn't carry much. But I only need the one credit card. That should be quite enough," Stan said quietly, holding a bankcard in his hand. Taking out the driver's license, the scientist looked at the picture. He would have to style his mane differently. Evan's hair went to the side. He hoped his cowlick wouldn't create a problem in that capacity. He supposed that the plan was reliable enough to work. His science had won out this time. In two weeks a trial would begin; the trial to put away a man who did not commit the rape of Melanie Crawford. He would be privileged enough to sit in the jury, as Mr. Evan Garrison Jurney. Stan loved the name as his own. No one would suspect or be the wiser.

The scholar was exhausted. Lying down on the mattress, his eyes closed, in peace.

The patrolman called in the license plate number. It hadn't been reported stolen. But he had a bad feeling. Something drew him to the car. It appeared that no one was inside, but intuition got the best of him. He ambled up with a swagger resembling Barney Fife. With caution, he opened the car door and looked inside. Though clean, something was definitely wrong. There was a strong scent causing his nose to wrinkle and his mouth to frown in digust. He couldn't tell if it was chemical or the stench of blood, though it smelled like a combination of the two. There was no stain in the front seat, but as he got nosier, searching the back seat, he saw it.

The seat had a small dried black-red patch. He scooted out of the seat and quickly made it back to his patrol car. "Officer needs assistance at Highway 320 west bound. Car abandoned, possible blood on the scene."

It wasn't very long before the car rolled in with lights, but no siren.

"Where is it? What do you think it is?" Leroy asked. He was all business but didn't like to take things too seriously. He figured this was a false call. It had to be a dumped car that was stolen.

"I'll let you see what you think. It's small but you won't be able to miss it." Bart escorted Leroy to the white sedan and they both peered in, Bart leaning over Leroy's shoulder. "You mind, Bart?"

Bart backed off, still maintaining a good view inside the vehicle. "Yeah, I see that. It's got to be called in for the crime unit to investigate. Hey, what do you imagine this stuff is?" He tried to pick it off the seat. It was rubbery, but stuck like super-glue. "Man, I can't get it off. Weird color, huh? Kind of like skin. Oh, heck. I'll hand this over to the trained employees and they can try to get it off the seat." He backed himself out of the car, shut the door and radioed the situation in. Within a few minutes, many more cars, marked and unmarked filed in and pulled over to the shoulder. When that was full, others pulled to the median. People mulled around, but only about half were actually collecting information.

One man gave out orders. "We need to treat this like we have a crime scene, guys. The spot in the seat showed up blood. There may be a body somewhere. Let's begin with a fifty-yard radius of the area. If someone dumped him, the dogs will catch the scent. Let's get going." Men in jackets with their unit printed on the back scurried out into the grassy field and woody areas around the interstate. Dogs led the way, but never found the scent they were hunting. The scavengers were frustrated and the dogs became tired. After some time had passed, they packed it up and went on their way.

Doctor Boone, the chief medical examiner, had collected the material around the bloodstain and prudently took the material with the unusual substance stuck to it. His lab would analyze and analyze again.

The investigators stopped when the tow truck pulled Evan's car to the police station for impounding.

Inside the lab, the blood was being tested for a DNA match. The computer worked and worked. They were used to taking their time on these things, since the equipment was ancient. The flexible, flesh colored substance was run through several tests to break down its makeup. The staff worked diligently on the case file with excitement. Typically this kind of crime was seen in the big cities, but in this town, it was dreadfully unusual. Everyone in the office had to admit they enjoyed it. No one knew for a fact that there was a murder, or even a bloody nose or a scratched knee. No one knew for a fact that the car was abandoned because it was stolen. Since nobody called it in stolen, it was very perplexing.

Work was done at the quickest pace possible. However, due to the small amount of sophisticated equipment they used, most of it had to be sent out to more advanced labs. It would take a couple of weeks before all of the results would be returned to them and by that time, the whole situation could be over and explained. They hoped, with an eccentric desire that this would begin a really exciting case.

The office ran efficiently. Glenn knew he could expect things to be done in a timely manner and done to perfection. Sarah handed him a file with the name Gabe Shaw written on the top.

"Thanks. I'll be in my office." He hastened to read the goods that Sarah was able to find out about the alleged rapist. He held information that the prosecuting attorney would need to use. He knew that the prosecutor's office was so swamped that a case such as this one could end up being taken lightly. He also knew that Margaret would do anything she could to beat him at the game, as it was to her. He just wanted results that would put the man responsible behind bars.

His desk was not cluttered. It was usually in perfect condition. Everything had a place and it was in such a manner that he didn't even have to look to pick up something he needed. The file lay open on the desk mat as he read the biography of the alleged pervert.

Gabe Michael Shaw, born 1/19/80 in Beaumont, TX. Parents…he got bored with the information. He needed to know the real stuff. He turned the page and looked at a short rap sheet, which showed only a few prior offenses.

He had a warrant for his arrest in '93 for speeding tickets, a felony charge of robbery and trespassing, and one misdemeanor of lewd behavior in public. He served two years of a four-year sentence for the felony. Released for good behavior.

"Hmmm. That doesn't seem like a bad rap sheet, at least not enough to prove that he was capable of raping a woman. Of course, the lewd behavior may be good to use in court." He sounded a bit optimistic.

"Sarah, can you fax this to Dave Mushane at the courthouse? Make sure it's confidential. His personal fax is in the Rolodex. Don't just fax it to the office. Put a note that I thought he could use the information I have underlined. Have him call me if he needs to discuss anything or tell him that I'll see him next Tuesday in court."

She could handle anything, no matter how detailed. She rushed out right away and did just as she was asked.

Glenn sat back in his leather seat and opened his mouth for a yawn. He needed peace and guidance. "Lord, I know you can hear me. Hear my need for the ability to remain calm. I am so nervous about this case. I'm not working it, but I feel so responsible for it to go our way." Suddenly, he couldn't wait for the trial.

If anyone asked Jason how he felt about Melanie, his answer would definitely be love. However, he was questioning her anger toward God. He understood the anger to an extent. He was mad too. But, she went further than that. She blamed God. If she needed to blame someone it couldn't be God. Although he did drop her off in the park that horrific night, Jason knew that she would never blame him. He still felt she could even be mad at him, but not the Lord. He wished that she would look to God for guidance and peace. She just couldn't leave God. Her faith had to return. He wouldn't, couldn't be with her if she left God. His prayers were for his heart to understand and be able to accept her. He prayed that she would return to her Lord and that the experience would have made her stronger in the relationship. It was too important to her, to them.

The same thoughts went through his head, over and over. He stared up at the ceiling in his room and listened to his roommate rummage through doors and gather up books and scattered papers.

"You ever getting up?" he asked.

"I thought about it. I need to go to my class, but I just don't feel like getting out of bed today. Oh, well." He sighed and pulled his feet up and laid them on the cold hard floor. He sat up and stretched.

Grabbing a pair of shorts and a clean T-shirt, he started out the door. On his way out, he pushed a navy blue baseball cap on his mussed hair and put a piece of gum in his mouth. Halfway down the hall, he realized that something was missing. He raced back to the room and picked up a history book for his class.

He made it just in time. His professor was known for locking the door when class started. Just as he sat down, the door was locked and the teacher began his lecture promptly. Jason was focused. He had to pass this summer school class to finish his history requirements for graduation.

"Please open your books to page 235. Who can tell me what year the Irish Potato famine began?" No one answered but pages flipped loudly. Class continued after an answer from the back was given. Jason was soaking in the information and his mind didn't wander to the events in his own life.

When class finished, the room emptied quickly and Jason followed. He was not in the mood to go back to his room. The pay phone was near so he dialed Abby.

"Abby, Good-morning."

"Hi, Jason. Melanie's not here right now."

"I know, but really I wanted to talk to you. It's been difficult having conversations with her lately and..."

"Honey, she has been through a lot and it will take some time before it's all normal. Well, normal isn't right. Give her some space. Let her talk to you when she's ready."

"No, it's not that. It's God. She's so mad at God. She has said things that make me think she's letting Him go. I know it sounds crazy but I am not reading into it, Abby. She blames Him and refuses to allow His grace to fall on her."

"I don't know what to say, Jason. It's not easy to go through something like she's been through and return to the same way of life. She's been wounded and she is frightened. She faces things everyday that will remind her of that night, and she will for the rest of her life. I know she loves God and I don't think that the anger is wrong. She's not directing it at Him."

"Yes, she is. I just wanted you to pray for her. I know how much you and she have talked lately and she's so fortunate to have you. I'm obviously not going to completely understand as much as a woman would. But, Abby, she's not herself. She's bitter and cold to the *name* of God, so I know she won't *pray* to Him."

"Hmmm. I didn't notice it, but I'll certainly try to be aware of it and if I can discuss it with her, maybe we can get down to some feelings and shatter a wall that she may be putting up. Jason, don't worry. It will all be fine. Like I said, give her some time. Don't push her."

The phones hung up on both ends. Both leaned their heads on the phone receiver and began to pray a similar prayer.

"Well, God, if two or more come together and pray..." Jason thought aloud, while he walked back to his room. It didn't bother him if others noticed the conversation he was having with himself. He somehow felt a bit of comfort knowing that there was another prayer going up on Melanie's behalf.

He would see her later that afternoon. They would do the usual; go have coffee and then go back to the school library to finish Jason's studies or Melanie would read a book. It was all so comfortable for them, in the past. The comfort-zone was threatened.

"Margaret, I have a meeting with Gabe Shaw's arresting officer scheduled for you in two hours."

"Thank you, Gail." Margaret was completely uninterested in anyone else but herself. However, this case would make a huge impression on the law firms that had previously scoffed at her ability to work for them. She was a joke to most firms. Her record of cases won was about twelve out of two hundred. She had to prove herself. Going up against Glenn would either make her or break her.

"Gail, can you help me with something?" She seemed a little more subdued than normal. What did she want?

"Yes, ma'am." Gail sat in a hard chair waiting to hear the request. She was positive that it would mean she would have a long night ahead of her.

"Gail, I've been looking over the arrest record. It's hard for me to see that this is credible, considering that there was really no physical evidence pointing to Gabe. The man was arrested for sexual assault. That I see. But, look at the way he was identified. The only one identifying him was Melanie Crawford and she couldn't see him. That's just a little puzzling to me. I don't think that should be admissible. It's not conclusive."

"What do you want me to do?"

"I *need* to talk to the lady again, who was assaulted. She obviously saw him, and even knew him. Why didn't Melanie? I know something is wrong with this. Glenn can't possibly think this is enough to charge someone with rape. Assault was a given but only on the other girl. Melanie didn't know who did it. She guessed at a voice. That's so ridiculous." Her finger tapped nervously on the desk creating a beat that resembled rain tapping on a window pane.

"So, what do you want me to do?" She was getting annoyed at her boss.

"I don't really know if we can change the plea or bargain down. If we have to go to trial, my best bet is to make the credibility of Melanie's line-up look as stupid as I think it really is. What I need you to do, I don't really know. Gail, get me something that can change the way this trial will go. Glenn is powerful and most of the jury would rather agree with someone like him than do the right thing. I think the only thing that might work is to make sure that the alibis are solid. Maybe Gabe has a great alibi." Her lip curled up at the corner knowing that it was a fat chance someone would help this low-life pervert out.

"You haven't spoken to him yet?"

"Well, I didn't really spend much time with him. I sat at the hearing and it went to trial. We didn't discuss anything about Melanie. I'm not even sure if he has an alibi for that evening." She slammed down her pencil with thousands of tiny teeth marks. She bit her upper lip and looked up at Gail. "Okay, I'm going to the police department. I'll be back later."

"Remember that you are meeting with the arresting officer in two hours." Margaret acknowledged Gail with a nod and slid out of the office quickly. Her long, thin legs clicked down the hallway out into the street loudly. Her strong perfume continued to linger. She was on her way to discredit Glenn Crawford. If she didn't, she would give it her best shot.

The policewoman at the desk led her to a long room with booths and a phone in each. A large glass window separated the hall with another that looked just the same. Same booths, same phones. Margaret sat down and tapped her pen on her notebook. She waited only a few minutes before she saw a young, medium height scruffy brown head come towards her. His orange outfit gave him a look of toughness, but he was scared. She smiled and he made no move to return the kindness. They picked up the phones and held the receiver to their ears.

"Who you?" he demanded. He knew.

"Margaret Ritchey, I'm your attorney."

"Well, *Miss* Ritchey. How are you going to get me out of here? You got something up your pretty little sleeves?" His face grinned hideously and scowled at her. He had no respect for women. She wondered why a man wasn't placed on this case. How could she defend someone who hurts women and feels no remorse? Oh well, this was her job and she absolutely hated it.

She looked at her paper and began to turn reports and read aloud. "It says you were arrested on assault charges. Tell me about that."

"She's just a broad I've been seeing for about a month. She's no one to me. I just got mad at her and it all just started happening. Things got out of hand. I would have stopped if I hadn't been stoned that night. She asked for some of it."

"Okay, so you admit to that. You also say you were intoxicated. What on? Crack, meth?"

"Just a wad of pot. It's all I could get my hands on that night. I ain't got a job, so I ain't got money. I do what I have to just to make a little dough. You know? Hey, but she was as stoned as me, Lady."

"Ms. Ritchey." She shuttered to think of the particular "jobs" he would have to take to cover his habit.

"Okay." He rolled his eyes.

"Well, what about March eighth? That was a Friday. Where were you?"

"What for? What's this about?" He looked confused, which gave Margaret a little more reason to think that this was not the rapist.

Her eyes shot him a look of genuine concern. He was completely stunned by the charge, giving her ample reason to pursue the truth. She knew that this was not the right man. She tried to explain. "The rape of Melanie Crawford. She was raped and she ID'd you in the voice line-up."

"Rape? I never raped my girl and I never raped no Melanie."

"So, if you didn't then do you remember where you were that night?" She got out a calendar and pressed it up to the window. He looked at it hard. "SO?" She pressed on.

"I think I was at my apartment. I got evicted sometime around then. I only owed for like five months. Yeah, my eviction was sometime around then. That's why I've been staying with friends. Then, I met Lonny. She's my girl right now." He put his head on his hand and listened to the receiver.

"The one you attacked? She's your girl? Why is she pressing charges if she's your girl?"

"She'll get over it."

"So you were being evicted? Could anyone corroborate your whereabouts that night? If you have a good alibi, it could stand to reason that the charges of rape will be dropped. Assault is still on you, I can't do much for that. The police report is pretty solid on that. Give me someone who can get you off for the other night."

"Like a dealer? Would that work?"

She sneered in awe of his ignorance. "I don't think it would be very smart to ask your dealer to present himself as an alibi. Think, Gabe. Who did you see that night?"

"Man, I don't know. I don't really remember that. It was two months ago, woman. How am I supposed to remember what I was doing or who I's with. That changes all the time."

She knew he was telling the truth. His lifestyle was pretty routine. The only thing not routine was that he would wake up in one place, buy some dope, and go plant himself somewhere else. Every night was pretty much the same. The location and people varied, but it was certainly predictable. The eviction could lead to something, though.

"Gabe, I hope you can remember something. I'm going to need the address and landlord. I'll follow that and see if it leads me anywhere."

"Dirk Longenbecker. He's German. Address is 14 Toole Street. Hey can you speak that?" He smiled a smile that showed his teeth, which resembled charcoal and butter. His teeth were filthy, if not rotten. She jotted down the name and didn't give Gabe any response to his absurd question. She hung up and walked away."Hey! Lady, you can't just hang up on me. Get me out of here!" he screamed through glass. She heard him but didn't look back.

Chapter 18

Jason stood waiting at the counter for a few minutes. The whirring and blending noises were comforting to him. The guy behind the counter put the lids on the cups and quietly walked to the cash register. He pressed keys and on the final one looked into Jason's eyes, "That will be five dollars and fourteen cents."

Jason noticed the odd look. It was looking deep into Jason and almost bore into him somehow. Jason smiled unevenly and brought out two five-dollar bills. The guy continued to look at him and then with a sudden move he stopped and said, "Thank you. Here's your change. I hope you enjoy it." He turned and went to work on another order.

Jason was puzzled but dismissed it as paranoia.

Melanie was sitting quietly in the booth as Jason made his way with two Lattes in his hand. He smiled at her and she smiled back. He sat down and nobody said anything. It was becoming awkward. They both knew that there was a tension and it was threatening both of them. The silence was uneasy and Melanie tried to open conversation.

"How was your day? Mine was pretty good. My eighteenth birthday is coming up. What are you going to get me?" She was kidding with him and he laughed, but she knew he was thinking of something else.

"I'm going to get you a small trinket. One that will remind you of me." His eyes looked hollow even through his sweet smile.

"Oh, so you're going to get me a trinket? Want me to guess?" She looked at him and her smile started to fade as she realized that he wasn't in the talking mood. "What's wrong, Jason? Why don't you talk to me?"

"Hey, I've got an idea. Why don't we go on to the library? Can we? I'd really like to start my studying early." They both rose and stepped outside the coffee shop. Jason threw his cup away which he had emptied quickly. Melanie continued to sip hers slowly.

"What's going on?" She wasn't dumb.

"I don't know. That guy in there looked at me like, I don't know."

"Maybe he knew you. Could you have gone to school with him a long time ago?"

"No, he was just weird."

They stifled conversation all the way to the library. Just as Jason shut the car door, his arms stiffened. His neck was forced up and his head began to rise as he was thrown into convulsions. Melanie screamed for help as a group of students ran over.

"Get him out of the car."

"No, you don't know how. You don't know what you're doing."

"911, we have an emergency. A guy is having a seizure. We're at the library at the university, in the parking lot. Come quick. No, he's in the car…I think his name is Jason. I don't know, hold on." He looked at Melanie, with haste, "Does he have any prior history of this?"

"No, he doesn't do this ever."

"No ma'am." He returned to the dispatcher.

Sirens were close by and soon the ambulance raced into the lot. Two men jumped from the front cab and one opened the back doors. "Let's get him out of the car."

The paramedics worked to get Jason's body stabilized as they monitored his pulse and checked his airway to make sure he wasn't swallowing his tongue.

Melanie sat in the back of the ambulance with Jason. She picked up her cell phone and dialed furiously.

"Mom, we're at the hospital. Jason just had a seizure. Get here quickly. Call Dad." She kept her hand on Jason's palm as she closed the phone and set it to her side. "What in the world could happen now? God, I see you have more in store for us." She talked quietly through gritting teeth.

Her heart longed so much for God's existence to be prevalent.

However, at this moment, she was sure that if He existed, it was only to torture her. She couldn't get past the idea that nothing had gone right for her in a while.

Jason's faith never wandered. He remained settled in the idea that God's love was faithful. He would never change his view of God. She knew that. It made her wonder if the relationship would be able to withstand the changes that were occurring.

His hand began to wiggle slowly and his eyes fluttered trying to open. She began to speak quietly to him with loving words and held his hand tighter as his grip became more taut. Finally she saw the whites of his eyes and then the brown. It was a miraculous moment for her to see him waken.

"Jason, I'm here." She held a smile on her face and he had to return the gesture, despite the fact that he remained weak and pale.

"Am I okay? I can't remember much," he said with hard deep breaths.

"I don't know what happened. You had a seizure and someone called 911. We should be at the hospital very soon. You haven't been unconscious long. We'll get you taken care of. I promise, we'll find out what is happening to you." She assured him, at the same time as she reassured herself as well.

The drive ended and the doors flew open as two men grabbed the rails and lifted the gurney out of the ambulance. A doctor and a couple of nurses rushed up and started taking vitals and rattling off other procedures that they would have to attend to in the emergency room.

"Ma'am you can wait out here." Without another word, they were gone and Melanie stood alone in a waiting room with several others. They all looked as lost as she did.

As soon as they could get there, Glenn and Abby arrived. Melanie filled them in and they all sat down on the hard orange chairs bolted to the walls. Nobody said anything. Nobody knew what to expect. Hours went by before anyone came out to give them information about what had taken place.

"Well, he's going to be fine, but I see he was just in about two months ago for an unexplained illness. The doctor who saw him then wrote down that he was sick from Rubidium. That's terribly unusual, but I'm going to check for that, as well as do a blood work-up for diabetes, hypoglycemia and epilepsy. It's going to be a while so I suggest you just go on and get some sleep." He turned and walked up to the desk flopping the chart in the file organizer. A cute nurse walked by and he made a remark that made her smirk as she touched the sleeve of his white coat.

Melanie walked up to him, tapped him on the shoulder while he turned around with a jerk. "Yes, ma'am."

"Can I go in to see Jason? I'm not leaving until I do." Glenn and Abby watched from the waiting room. When Melanie smiled at them, they knew she had permission to go to Jason. Rising from their seats, they followed Melanie to the room where Jason lay on his back with a few tubes coming out of his arms and nose. His eyes were closed but he opened them as soon as he heard the familiar voices in the room.

"Hey," he said weakly.

Melanie leaned over and kissed him on the cheek. "We have to stop meeting like this." They giggled but both were very concerned at the frequency of the hospital visits.

"What is going on with me?"

"We don't know. They haven't brought any of the tests back. It probably won't be until tomorrow when we find out."

"Jason, I'm becoming very worried about these incidences. It seems very peculiar that both times you became ill you and Melanie had been at the coffee shop. I wonder if you are allergic or something." Glenn probed for some explanation.

"I never was before. Why would it start right now? I've been going to that same coffee shop since it opened. And if I'm not allergic, why isn't Melanie getting sick? I don't think it's the coffee shop." Something inside him felt differently though.

"Well, maybe we will know something tomorrow. We aren't going to keep you up. You need to sleep."

"Are you leaving?" His voice was shaky and fearful. "Well, I guess you can't sleep in the waiting room. Will you come early?"

"Jason, I love you and I will be here when you wake up. I promise." Melanie leaned over and hugged him. When they walked away, Jason began a continuous prayer for answers, peace and understanding. He fell asleep while the words were coming out of his mouth.

"Margaret. Hi." The older man stood up and reached his hand over a desk piled high with files and papers. He didn't really know what much of it was, so he never made much effort to sift through it. "Please excuse my office. I've got so much busy work, but I have to admit, I'd rather be out in the field. I guess you want to talk about Gabe Shaw." His hand rummaged around for the case file and finally found it under his phone. "Aha! Here it is."

"Joe, I'm confused at some things. It isn't fitting together. Explain to me how Gabe Shaw is being charged with the rape of Melanie Crawford?"

"Well, that's a tricky one, but we know that she was raped. Margaret, you have to know that this type of thing doesn't happen in this town, ever. It also appears that she identified his voice. How can you explain that? Margaret, it's not really an airtight case, but you *have* to see the coincidence. When I arrested him, he wasn't belligerent and didn't want to speak. Consequently, he didn't defend himself. He just gave up. If he were innocent, he wouldn't have come in without some sort of protest. It's been my experience that the one's who yell the hardest and loudest are trying to clear themselves of false accusation."

"Ever hear of playing the game? Sometimes the quiet ones are the ones who are innocent, but intelligently don't talk to anyone but their lawyer. Did he say anything before you Mirandized him? Anything. I need something to go on. Joe, you got him for sexual assault, no question, but the connection to Melanie is way off for this guy. No motive. No real evidence. No admission to anything but the assault. He doesn't even know who she is. What have you really got, Joe?"

She was pushing for anything she could get that would help her win the case.

"Margaret, give some leeway here and think about the coincidence. Truthfully, we didn't have any evidence on him for the rape. It just seemed probable that one rape, in a town that has carried a clean record, would be miserable. But, when two occur, that's just too much of a fluke. It had to be him. The idea that there are two of these idiots out there sickens me."

Her head shook and her mouth thinned out as she spoke. "Joe, it's still not washing. And remember what you have him on is not rape. It's assault. He had an alibi for the evening of Melanie's rape. Did you check on that at all? I've got to make sure it's viable, but it's not going to help the prosecutor at all if I can get it done."

He raised his hands in surrender. "No, we didn't check his alibi for that evening. Our failure, but like I said, two in this town is not normal. Sure it happens in the bigger cities, everyday, but here? Margaret, you are a fair attorney so please look at it reasonably."

She looked down her nose at him. "I will, and when the evidence has proven him innocent, you will be very sorry for your lax judgement and procedure. Thank you, Joe. I will see you later." She turned on her heels and strolled out of his office.

Upon arrival at her car, she noticed a flyer or card on the windshield. Thinking it a cleaner's ad or a Church Bizarre invitation, she wadded it up but then noticed the handwriting. It was almost scribbled manuscript. She had a difficult time making out the words, all except one. "Died." Alarmed by the freakish note, she pulled her keys out of her bag and pushed them into the keyhole. Her car didn't have keyless entry, but she vowed that she would change that immediately. Getting into the driver's seat, her heart was pounding. She locked the door and felt her hands trembled while searching for the ignition. Her eyes scanned the area around her, not knowing what, or who she was looking for. She sped off with fear. Her next destination was the apartment complex where Gabe Shaw resided two months before.

The apartments were shanty and she wondered how anyone would think these were acceptable places to live. Kids with old raggedy clothes, no shoes and dirty faces wandered the street and hung on the stairs leading to the entrance of row houses. This was the first time Margaret had ever known this place existed in her town. How could she have not heard about this? She was shocked to realize that this area resembled a large city's ghetto. It was still daylight, so she wasn't too scared to get out and go inside.

The gray paint on the bricks was peeling off and pipes hung out of the bottom floors. They were rusty. Water dripped from them and it was just as rusty. Inside was worse. The carpet was yellow and green shag, with cigarette holes and odd colored stains. Walls had holes the size of fists; the pay phone didn't have a receiver, and the man behind the desk was sleeping with a bottle of whiskey in his lap. It had to be empty because it had turned over on its side and nothing was running out. She could only assume that this man would be the honorable landlord.

She tapped on the desk and his eyes slowly looked her direction. Not wanting to spend any more time there than she had to, she quickly spoke up.

"Margaret Ritchey, State Defense Attorney. I'm here to get some information on one of your tenants. He was evicted two months ago. Gabe Shaw. Do you remember him?"

"Who are you again?" He sat up, eyeing her with very little interest. "Who did you say you were looking for?"

"I'm not looking for anyone. I'm Gabe Shaw's attorney." Her irritation was obvious.

He jumped up with a spring in his step and suddenly became very sober as well as defensive. "That jerk owed me five months of rent. He didn't pay, so he got kicked out. I don't have to defend myself for that." He was defensive all the same. She expected a German accent but apparently he had been in America for a while.

"No, no. Not that kind of attorney. I'm a defense attorney and I need to know the whereabouts of Mr. Shaw on March the eighth. He was being evicted around that time, according to his memory. Can you corroborate the fact that he was here that evening?"

He thought for several minutes as his hand made circles on the desk. He was terribly jittery and Margaret assumed that the buzz was wearing off.

"Hey, I do think I remember him being here sometime that night because he got into it with some girl. She wanted a bag of clothes that she'd left in the apartment but he told her he torched 'em. She was furious mad. Yeah, I remember that. See that hole over there by the bulletin board? She did that. She was aimin' for his head." He was proud of his memory.

"Who was she? Do you have her name or a forwarding address?"

"Lady, she was just one of the women who walk in and outta here. She was hookin'. He probably tried to pimp her out and she left. When she came back to get her junk, he'd gotten rid of it."

"Do you know this for sure?"

"No, but it's usual around here. I do remember he called her Trina or Gina or something like that."

"Okay, thank you, Mr. Longenbecker." She excused herself and hurried to her car. She hoped no one had taken the tires or hubcaps. It looked fine so she got in, locked the door and pressed the gas pedal with force. She exited the area, having little intention of returning. Her car entered town and drove around the square where the jail was built. Her mission continued.

"Okay, Gabe, give it to me straight. Who is Trina or Gina?"

He sat across from her with the phone in his hand. "Oh, her?"

"Yeah, her. Who is she?" She spoke with strength and persistence. He got the idea she wasn't playing around.

"I was with her for a little bit of time and she turned out to be a loser. I got rid of her *and* her stuff. Why?"

"Where can I find her?"

"How the heck do I know? Gina wasn't even her real name. It's Grace Jernigan. She used Gina as a street name. Who'd want to pay for a girl named Grace?"

"How old is she?"

"Why does that matter?" He resented every question she brought to him, in spite of the fact that it was in his best interest.

"Because, Gabe, if she is a minor, you might have a problem with *statutory* rape charges if she testifies on your behalf."

"She's twenty. That's what she told me. How can she help me?"

"*If* she will, then maybe she can corroborate your claim that you were at your apartment. When you were fighting with her, the timing may be perfect. Gabe, I'll look for her. She's your best bet. The prosecutor is well respected but he has an even more powerful person behind him. You need to be straight with me, on everything. Let's just hope she has fond memories of you."

"Okay, Ms. Ritchey. But you gotta be straight with me too. How are you going to get me outta here?"

"No, no, no. You're still going to jail for the assault, but it's the rape charge that we want expunged. We can plea down for the assault, maybe get you off on less time."

"What is expunged?" She'd lost him on that word.

She began to stand up and put her notepad back into the briefcase, as she leaned over and spoke into the receiver, "Removed. Erased. I've got to go. I'll be in contact." She hung up and once again he sat with the phone receiver to his ear as she walked away. He felt so terribly vulnerable once again.

Glenn went home from the hospital and wondered how the climate would be, since he'd told his mom to leave. The back door was open and he could hear music coming from the yard.

"Mom, hey. Are you out there?"

"Hi Glenn. I'm doing some yard work. I noticed the weeds growing up in the flower bed and thought I'd try to get them picked so that you and Abby won't have to." Her hands were covered in soil and across her face were traces of dirt.

"Mom, are you fine?"

"Yes, I've just had a little time to think about things. You know, you are absolutely right. I shouldn't have come to your house and just taken over. I shouldn't have expected your family to replace your father. It's not fair to any of you to change your lives for my benefit."

"Well, I'm not going to argue with you, but I appreciate you taking this so graciously. I hope you will allow me to help you find a place.

I also hope that you know that you are welcome to visit anytime."

She didn't know if that was what she wanted to hear. Deep down she wanted Glenn to take back his request for her to leave. She knew it was true. She needed to leave and get on with her life. She thought to herself of all the activities she could engage in; bingo at the Y, water aerobics at the Y, church yard sales and bake sales. The list went on and on and she somehow started to feel better. Maybe she could be part of a bridge club.

Glenn started to return indoors but was caught once more. "Glenn, I'd like to go look tomorrow."

"Okay Mom. Thanks. I'm getting a sandwich, you want one?"

She nodded and he left for the kitchen.

Chapter 19

A diligent silence held the room as two laboratory workers stood over the bloody material waiting for a blood match that might give a name. If it came from someone who had been treated at one of the hospitals, they would have some luck. If not, the blood may as well have belonged to a dog or cat. It wouldn't matter. Luck would have its day.

"This is blood from a man named Evan Jurney. He has been reported missing by his workplace. You thinking foul play?"

"Yep, that's exactly what I think. They found the car and no body. Was he pulled over for some reason and randomly got snatched up by someone? I don't know. It doesn't fly with me. Let's get that other patch of material with the plastic stuff. We need to identify its make-up because I just have a feeling that it's going to help us figure out what happened."

"Done. I've divided up the substance into liquid and solid." She smiled, one step ahead of him.

"Oh good. What did you come up with?"

"I found something very odd. It's mask latex. However, it is not your typical latex. It contains Ethidium Bromide. Labs sometimes, but rarely anymore, use that to dye gels for DNA. It's known to be very toxic if not diluted. I wonder if there are any companies or factories that use this stuff in latex or if it was homemade."

"Ethidium Bromide? I haven't heard much about the use of it. How would anyone know to use it with latex unless they studied it extensively and knew its properties?"

"What are you getting at?"

"I'm thinking that we need to investigate the use of Ethidium Bromide in our city. It has to be shipped in if someone is making things with it. I just don't know how we can find out where it's coming from or where it's going to."

"You got me. I'd never heard of it before. Well, I have, I just didn't know what the other uses of it would be. I only heard of it in my chemistry classes."

"Yeah, me too." He sat with his chin on his fist. He had to think of something. "Research. I'm going to the Internet for some advice."

He picked up the analysis of the substance and made his way down the hall to search for information on his findings.

"Jason, I'm here. I told you I would be here first thing in the morning." She touched his hair and wiped it out of his eyes. He was still asleep so she sat on the edge of the bed and stroked his hand. Slowly his eyes opened one at a time. A smile crossed his mouth and she smiled back.

"Thank you for taking care of me. I slept all night, I guess. I don't remember waking up."

"How do you feel?"

"I'm feeling much better. The lab results in yet?"

She sighed with disappointment. "I don't know, but I would say no. I don't think the doctor has even come in this early."

"Do you realize that both times I've been sick we had just been at the coffee shop. Your dad thinks that it's connected, but I have to admit that I think it's weird, too. Do you? I mean, think about it. The coffee shop *was* the common factor considering I'm not prone to having seizures or fainting spells."

"You know, that *is* really strange. But if it's the coffee, why didn't I get sick? It seems like a stretch thinking it might be food poisoning or just very bad coffee."

"No, that's not what I'm thinking of. Maybe something is deliberate. It could be done on purpose. But I don't know why it would be aimed at *me*." He was becoming energized at the possibility of criminal activity. It was exciting albeit frightening and far-fetched.

"You have a little more imagination than I do. Why would anyone want to get to you? And why would God allow anything more to happen to us? Has it not been enough for Him?" She appeared agitated as she stood and walked toward the window. Jason was concerned by the remarks and remembered the same type of comments since her rape occurred.

The curtain was drawn until she pulled the cord allowing a cloudy day to rear its head in the room. Even the clouds gave a little light in the dark room with icy, white walls, but it did nothing to warm up the climate that was developing. She had opened the door to a conversation that neither wanted to pursue.

"What did you mean by that? I've heard you say a lot of things like that lately and Mel, I'm worried about you. What is going on in that head of yours?" Jason pressed without caution.

"What? Am I not allowed to have feelings?" Her voice was nearly yelling.

"No, that's not what I'm talking about and you know it. Are you fighting God right now?"

"Fighting? Why fight when I keep losing anyway? You should know better than anyone what I've been through. I was raped. I may never have children. That's still up in the air. I've been stalked. Let's see, what else? I'll have to go to court soon to put someone behind bars. I have to keep bringing you to the hospital for unknown reasons. Why should I even care what God has to do for me? He has done nothing!"

Jason remained collected. "It's not right for you to ignore God's voice when you know good and well that He's talking to you. You don't give me any pity party. I won't listen to it and frankly, I don't think you are all that mad at God. I think you are just scared and upset. It's okay. I can accept that."

Melanie broke in with anger shooting from her eyes and fire from her tongue.

"Well, I'm certainly glad *you* can accept it. Lord knows I've worried all this time how you could accept this. Jason, you go on and on about God's voice talking to me. You know what I'm hearing? I hear, 'Melanie, I was faithful to you for so many years and now, I have to go.' Maybe He plans to check on me later." Jason motioned for her to come to him. She nodded, no. He held out his arm and she could not ignore him. She fell into his arms, with tears of fear and anxiety.

"I'm sorry. I know I haven't told you that I *don't* know how you feel. I think you have heard me say the wrong things. Let me try again. Sure, you have the right to be mad and you have every right to question why. I want you to hear the voice that gives us peace. Until you let the barrier down, just a little, you won't hear anything but anger. That's coming from you. Melanie, sweetie, you are stronger than this. Don't let Satan pull a sheet over your eyes and show you the wrong way to handle things. When God lets us feel emotions, it's not wrong. Jesus Christ felt every emotion. How angry must he have been at the illegal trials and pain inflicted on him? God was faithful then and He will be now." She pressed her face in the curve of his neck and cried several minutes.

As she pulled away, she nodded. "You're right. I haven't been faithful to Him. I can't believe I didn't know how to handle this, any of this. It's not like me to abandon my beliefs. God, please forgive me. Oh, I'm so sorry. I love you so much."

Their hands intertwined in a hard grip. Together their relationships with God would grow stronger.

A knock on the door interrupted the reunion of minds and hearts.

The doctor peeked in and asked if he could interrupt for a moment. He carried the chart that held possible answers to their questions.

"Jason, how do we feel this morning? Before you answer that, let me just say that you get to go home after I talk to you. Okay, so?"

"I'm feeling fine. What happened to me?"

The doctor's lip mouth frowned with a bit of discouragement at the answer. "Rubidium. It was in your file that they found traces of it in your blood the last time you were in. I had the lab check for this and sure enough, that's what they found. The only problem is that the amount of the element was far more than previously. I don't know what else to tell you."

"So, did it come from the coffee shop?"

"Pardon? How did you know about coffee?"

"That's what we were told before. Coffee, tea and tobacco. Right?"

"Yeah, you got it. It's not found in large amounts usually, but it can be very dangerous, as you have found out, twice." The doctor smiled and his eyes showed his age as the lines framed them. He was a very handsome man and had a sincere look about him. With concern, he asked, "Have you had coffee lately? I mean, have you had any signs of allergic reactions or possibly noticed something funny after you drink a cup?"

Jason became agitated at the worry, which was beginning to show evidence of something more than just bad coffee or a strange reaction. Was something more sinister? He wondered if this began a chain of new events.

"I got my coffee at the shop on the corner of Main and First. I remember getting the same coffee the time before, at the same place. The same people always work in there."

Something was bringing him to the frightening realization that this was not coincidental. Jason grabbed Melanie's hand and looked at her strongly.

"Do you remember anything that was weird when we were there?"

She didn't pause even a moment. "No."

"No, Mel, think. Think hard. It's not right. I have a feeling that this was supposed to happen to me."

The doctor popped in with his opinion on the matter. "Now, Jason, I don't want you to start looking into things on your own. Though the cause is very unusual, it would be safer to let the police look into anything that could be harmful. I'll send the information to the medical examiner and see if they can come up with a logical explanation."

"Jason, I agree. If it's something deliberate, you certainly don't need to get involved any more than you are."

Melanie was still apprehensive at the thought of more than coincidence. Why would anything happen to Jason? She couldn't allow herself to see any reason for harming him. She was completely blind to the possibility.

"Jason, you need to do what I'm advising. It's not wise for you to put yourself out there if it's dangerous. I mean it. Let's just see what comes up next." He turned to leave and then stopped. His eyes smiled as he laughed, "Oh, and Jason, no more coffee. Doctor's orders." He exited leaving a confused young couple with unanswered questions.

"What do you think, Mel?"

"I think you think too much. Just come on and be real. You can't honestly think this is a big deal."

"My seizure wasn't a big deal? I'm sorry, I thought that my health was of great importance to you."

"Oh, don't be silly. It was serious but I think you are overestimating the real issue."

"Which would be?"

"The real issue is that you are alive, safe and most of all, I love you." She grinned and leaned over, kissing him on the forehead. He was still unconvinced of his well-being.

Glenn stood in front of his desk, waiting for a reaction from Margaret at the evidence she was trying to produce. She looked nervous as she fished around in her briefcase for the files on Gabe Shaw.

"Margaret, did you leave it at your office?"

"No." She was irritated at his insensitive ridicule of her. "Glenn, I have several cases on the burner and I happen to keep them all in this attaché case." He was amused at her use of the word attaché. She always did try to be bigger than she was. She suddenly pulled out the small file. "Aha! Here it is…"

"It's awfully small. Do you have much that will help your client?"

"Well, I'll let you see. I have not spoken to a girlfriend that my client had during your daughter's rape. I have explained that he can't contest the assault since the police caught him in the act. He understands that but he really doesn't seem to know anything about the rape of your daughter. By the way, isn't this going to be a conflict of interest for you? You know you can't possibly represent her and be fair in the courtroom."

He ignored her comment. "So, you don't have anything to prove he didn't rape her?"

"Glenn, did you hear what I said?"

"Yeah, I'm not representing her. I'm supporting her while Dave Mushane carries the case. I am, however, asking for you to give me the low down on what you have that will provide your client with an alibi. I assume you don't have much, if anything."

"I'm working on the girlfriend idea. I have to say it's difficult to find a junkie or a hooker."

"You should know a lot of hookers. You represent them all the time, don't you? No, I'm sorry. That was rude and I apologize. I have to admit, you are handling a tough case and I do see your diligence. Well, Margaret, I must get back to work, so if you don't mind..."

"Yeah, sure. No problem. I just drove over here for a skinning anyway."

"A skinning? That was hardly a skinning. I merely made a point of noticing that you didn't have adequate evidence to show your client's innocence in the rape. We don't have too many crimes like this so I think nobody will find it to be a coincidence."

"Okay, I will go. Apology accepted. I will notify you if I get a witness." She slipped out past Sarah, who was entering to notify Glenn of his next appointment.

"Dave Mushane is here to see you."

Dave passed Margaret and smiled a sly smirk that warned her of his armor in court.

"Dave, hey man. What's the news?"

"Well, I have looked over the facts you sent me on Gabe Shaw. The lewd behavior could be used to show a lack of good judgement, which we could present as a rising pattern of behavior, resulting in assault and rape. The rape charge may not stand though. The evidence isn't there. The rape kit showed no fluids. There were no skin or hair samples in her fingernails. We really don't have anything other than the tape of his voice. It's a good thing she identified him in the line-up or you'd really have nothing. Besides, be grateful that there is a sex assault charge on the table. He *will* be put away."

Glenn bowed his head and rose from leaning on his desk. He

walked around and put his hands on the back of his leather chair. "Yeah, I know, but that isn't enough time. I want him there a lot longer than he's going to get. He'll get off with a slap on the hand as far as the sentence is concerned if the one charge is all that you really have."

"Well, Glenn, I wish I had more to tell you. You know I do. See you tomorrow."

The case was coming too quickly and for the first time, Glenn felt pressure. He was not the attorney, but he felt the clamps gripping him tightly. It was more than a case. It was a mission. He wondered if they did have the right guy, though. He wanted so badly to believe that it was Gabe Shaw. Tomorrow would come way too quickly.

Margaret walked into the office and glared at Gail who was waiting on a fax and eating a sandwich at the same time. She was used to eating in the office. Lunch usually didn't happen.

"Gail? Do you have the address or phone number?"

She knew who she was referring to. "You should thank me, Margaret. I am everything you needed in this office. Yes, I found her. She's working at a low-life bar outside town. You know where the projects were? Keep going that direction. It's not far out of there."

Handing the address on one page and the mug shot on another, Gail hoped this would prove her abilities, and get her in better graces with her boss. It wouldn't.

"Thank you, now let's see if you can find anything on the Graham file?" She grabbed the papers and set out of the office for the lower part of town that was now becoming a regular haunt for her. She loathed her job. Gail loved hers, but she despised Margaret.

The drive was pleasant enough and then she began to pass broken down houses, slabs where buildings used to stand, and absolutely no trees to speak of. She was in the projects. She continued to drive further and noticed a couple of ladies sitting on the front stoops with beers and brooms. As she began to leave the area, the trees appeared again. One, two, three. They were there, but they were very few and far between. A loud thumping noise was rattling her car as she approached a metal building with the window in the door blackened to hide the goings-on. She pulled into the parking lot, which held three trucks, and two land barges.

"Why didn't I bring anyone with me? Marge, you have got to get off your high-horse and take help when you need it." She unbuckled her seat belt, pulled the keys out of the ignition and remembered that she had a nine-millimeter in her purse, should it come down to that. "Well, here goes."

She stood out like a sore thumb. The darkness wasn't completely dark. The disco ball hung in the middle of the room with dark, filthy carpet and several chairs lined up along a stage. She prayed that the show would hold off until she had escaped the den of sin, as she would refer to it from that point on. She ambled up to the bar and held up a picture to two men who seemed too inebriated to see straight.

"Have you seen her? I need to find her."

"Nope, I ain't seen her. Can't say I wouldn't want to though, hmm hmm."

His breath wakened her senses even more. She was repulsed. "No, okay, go back to your business." She turned and motioned for the bartender to assist her.

"What's your drink, Lady? You sure you in the right place?"

"Yeah, I hope so. I'm not drinking. I'm looking for a girl named Grace Jernigan."

"Nope, not a name I know." He turned and wiped off a glass that was covered in brown liquid that she could only assume was alcohol. He didn't wash it; he just wiped it off. She was incensed and growing nauseated by the minute.

"No, sir, I need to find her. She may go by the name Gina."

He turned around and asked, "What do you need her for?"

"So you know her?"

"I didn't say that, I'm just being curious. What do you need her for?"

"I am representing her ex in a case and she could help him out by being his witness or alibi for the evening in question. So? Did I win approval? You gonna tell me the truth?" She was getting tougher and bolder in her questioning.

"If I get her, you ain't gonna turn this place into a war zone?"

"I promise, I only want to talk to her. No cops, nothing."

"Yeah, that's her. She's about to go on stage. Can you wait till she's finished? I got paying customers here."

"Okay." She regretted saying that from the minute the words came out of her mouth. Margaret was already uncomfortable, but now she had to watch a strip show. "The things I do for this job. It's really not worth it." She sat down in a chair and refused to touch the table with her hands. She held her head down the entire time the dance went on. When the music waned, she looked up and caught a glimpse of Gina grabbing her clothing and scooting off the stage. She waited and Gina appeared with a robe on and a cigarette hanging on her bottom lip as she mouthed to the bartender, "Her?" She meandered over to Margaret and sat down putting her cigarette out on the table surface.

"You wanted to see me, Lady?" She was high and wreaked of pot mixed with liquor. It was a disgusting mix.

"Hi, I'm Margaret. I represent your boyfriend Gabe Shaw."

"Ex. He's not my boyfriend. He's a lush."

"Okay, ex. We need an alibi for him on March the eighth. A rape occurred and he has been charged with it, along with sexual assault of his new girlfriend."

"Yeah, that's about right. He would do that. He tells you he loves you and then hits you to show you how much. He's out of luck. I won't help him. I don't care if he rots in jail. You tell him that, okay?"

She stood up, popped her knuckles and walked away. She turned back around, "Hey, you like the show?"

"Yes, you were stunning. Look, I really wish you would consider talking to me. Please?"

"What's in it for me? If I am his alibi, what do I get, and please don't say him?"

"I will see about getting you some help."

"For what? I don't need no help. I just need a crib to crash on and some more bikinis for work. You know?"

"Alright, I will take you shopping at Wal-Mart for some clothes, but you can't stay at my house."

"Yeah, yeah. So, when was this?"

"March eighth. Were you living with him at the apartments then?"

"What month is this?"

Margaret rolled her eyes and thought, *You have really fried your brain.* She said aloud, "It's July, summer. Do you remember back that far?"

"Hey, you ain't gotta get nasty with me. I stayed with him through winter and some of spring. So, I may have been with him in March. I don't remember days, that's a lot to ask."

"But do you remember hitting a hole in the wall? Do you remember Gabe telling you that he burned all of your clothes? Does any of this ring a bell?"

"Yes, it does. I don't know if that was the eighth, though. What day is that?"

"It was a Friday."

"Yeah, he burned every single one of my outfits for work. He knew it cost a lot to get new ones. He almost made me lose my job."

"The time of evening is crucial. Were you fighting around midnight?"

"Yes, or maybe it was ten. I remember getting off work and sometimes I get off around ten."

"Do you just come home?"

"Sometimes. Sometimes I get sauced or high. I don't know when I come home then."

Margaret was getting nowhere and she assumed that maybe this would be enough to present in court. It would be easier if the details were consistent and valid. Junkies, hookers, addicts, she was in a horrible world that couldn't see an out any other way.

"Well, thank you, Gina. I appreciate your help."

"When are we going shopping?" Her gum nearly fell out of her mouth as she smacked and spoke simultaneously.

Margaret looked around for a way out but then thought it best to get it out of the way. Checking her watch, she looked up and smiled,

"I'll take you now, if you can. This would be the best time for me."

Gina yelled across the entire room, "Vernon, I'm gonna get some new outfits. Be back in a while." He nodded with little care.

This is what Margaret wanted to do. She looked forward to finding the smallest bikinis on earth with a girl like this. They drove away for their big outing.

Chapter 20

The lab technician scanned the fax coming in from the doctor's office. "Rubidium? That's an interesting one."

He read over the report that detailed the amounts of Rubidium found both times in Jason's system. The doctor had written a note on the back that read,

This patient never had symptoms or episodes of seizures until recently. Both times, he had been drinking coffee. Is it possible that this amount of Rubidium that may be found in coffee, or is it possible that foul play has taken place?

Please look into this, I find it very suspicious.

Gary Harburk, MD

"Mmm." The technician stood over the papers and became puzzled. "How in the world did this much get in this guy's system?" He wondered aloud, grabbing the attention of his partner.

"What've you got there?"

"Look at the levels of Rubidium in this guys blood. It's a wonder he's still alive. Maybe they got him to the hospital in time to stop the effects, but my guess is that he had one major seizure. I just can't figure how that much was found. The doctor who sent this over wants me to check and figure out if this was foul play. By looking, I'd say definitely. It's normal to have small, minute traces in coffee, which they said he had been drinking, but this amount had to be deliberate. It's way too concentrated."

The partner listened intently and then proceeded to write a note to the doctor letting him know that there was ample reason to believe that something more was going on than just a bad cup of coffee. This was beginning to be a very full load of work lately. The latex, the Rubidium, blood of a missing man, what next?

"Hey, I got a list of the suppliers of Ethidium Bromide. It ships from several companies but only one ships to our city. It goes straight to the university. Science classes, primarily chemistry classes make use of it."

"Well, now we know where to start looking for latex. I have a feeling that if we find the latex, we find its creator. This is an odd way to make it. Someone knows a lot about what he's doing to create something this obscure. I'll tell the detectives on the missing case that something may be leading to the university chem labs. It's getting so exciting. Don't you think?" He rolled his chair over to the microscope and grinned like the Cheshire cat, then lowered his eyes onto the eyepiece. "This is so cool."

The courtroom was quiet for a while as Glenn and Abby walked in with Melanie and Jason following. Melanie's hands shook fiercely as they family made their way to the front row of pews behind the prosecution's table. She wasn't sure she could do this. It seemed too unbelievable and yet she so wanted to see him go away for hurting her.

The attorneys from both sides came in through the doors. Glenn looked back as Dave Mushane walked in front of Margaret. She looked distressed. Dave looked firm and confident, as usual. They all nodded in each other's direction as Glenn rose to shake Dave's hand.

Margaret passed and made a left to her table with her briefcase. She unloaded the pack and flipped through files. Her only wish was that she could have talked Gina into appearing on behalf of her client. Maybe the alibi would give the jury enough reason to doubt. That was all she really needed anyway; a pinch of doubt. They can't convict him if they don't know for sure. "Of course," she reasoned to herself, "they have done it before. They could do it again. Why not? He's a low-life."

She picked up a pen and scribbled a note stating that she had found the alibi for Gabe Shaw and that she was presenting that information to the jury for consideration for dismissal. She passed it quietly to Dave. Glenn stood up and read over Dave's shoulder. They both looked over at her as she smiled gloatingly at them both. Dave nodded and simply said, "Give it your best shot, Marge. You know that hearsay doesn't hold up in a courtroom. Without the actual witness, you have nothing."

Her smile turned to a pout and she turned her head away quickly. She knew he was right. The judge wouldn't allow it to be presented. Now what?

More people filed in, in droves, including Lonny and the police officers that stopped her attack. Soon the room buzzed with whispering voices. It sounded much like beehive. The jury was escorted into their seats at the right of the room. Amongst the jury was Evan Jurney. No one in the courtroom had a clue that the man was reported missing. Stan was lucky in that capacity.

As the judge entered, everyone rose in respect and waited for his command to sit down. Everyone sat and the proceedings began.

Stan looked through his new eyes and stared at Melanie. She didn't notice. She had her eye on Gabe Shaw. Stan wondered what Jason was doing there. What had happened? He was supposed to have been too sick to be there. Oh, well. That didn't matter. He was excited over his seat for the show.

She was radiant. Her wounds had healed well and the fear in her eyes was a pleasant reminder of the night he had with her. Her hand reached over to Jason's and they grasped tightly.

Stan wrung his hands in anger. The lady next to him was enthralled in the courtroom banter but looked disturbed at the odd behavior of the jury member beside her. For the first time, she noticed he had a strange texture to his face and she summed it up to burns or horrible acne as a teen. He grunted and then smiled at her, so she crossed her legs, turned away from him and made no effort to look at him again.

Questioning began and continued a short while relating to the sexual assault of Gabe's girlfriend. It was no contest on that charge. The possibility of Gabe committing the rape was more vague, so more questions were needed of the people involved.

Melanie appeared on the bench and spoke frankly. Her answers were precise and quick. She continued to be oblivious to the juror who couldn't take his eyes off of her. No one else seemed to notice it either.

Stan stared deeply at her as did the rest of the jury, but his was out of a hateful love. He noticed how shaky her voice became at times and wondered if the memories were as strong in her mind as they were in his. He assumed so. He became angry as the questions to Melanie came to an end. *Why so soon?* he wondered.

More probing of different people held the jury's attention well. It was then that Gabe Shaw was called to the stand.

"Mr. Shaw, can you tell us where you were the night of March 8?" Margaret had coached him on his answer.

"Yes, sir. I was at my apartment fighting with my ex-girlfriend, Grace Jernigan. I didn't do nothing about no rape."

He pleaded to the judge as Margaret rose immediately, "Your honor?"

"Mr. Shaw, please answer the questions. Jury will be asked to ignore the last statement made by the defendant."

Dave continued, "So, you were fighting with your girlfriend?"

"Ex."

"Sure. Is it characteristic of you to physically fight with each of your girlfriends?"

"Huh?"

"Let me ask you this. Do you fight women often?"

"No, only when they get stupid. Grace was a junkie, and Lonny made me steaming mad. I just did what I had to do." Gabe looked at Margaret who was brooding over the answers her client gave. His eyes begged her for a better answer. There were none.

"You say you do what you have to do? Was it possible that the night of March eighth, when you *say* you were with your *ex*...," Dave looked at him to acknowledge the use of ex, "that you possibly were so riled up that after the argument, you left the scene? Maybe took a walk to cool off?" Dave gave a shrug of his shoulders as he asked the question to give a possible absence of alibi to the defendant.

Gabe didn't budge. He knew he wasn't guilty of that rape. He spoke straightforward, which was much more intimidating to Dave than he expected.

"No, I didn't. I went to my apartment and shut the door."

Dave had to rework his interrogation since he was becoming convinced that the defendant might be telling the truth. He dismissed that thought as soon as it entered his mind.

"You remember that or did your attorney advise you of that?"

Margaret rose again, steaming, "Objection, your Honor!"

"Sustained. Mr. Mushane, stay with the questioning."

"Ok, your Honor, no further questions." He sat down.

Margaret walked to the jury box and stood facing the jury as she directed her questions to Mr. Shaw.

"You have established the fact that you were not in the park the night of Melanie Crawford's rape. Is that correct?"

"I said that." She shot him a look of annoyance. He looked right at her and got the message.

"Just a yes or no, please. You seem to fight quite a bit, Mr. Shaw. In your statement, you made the point of saying that you were fighting with an ex-girlfriend on the night of March eighth. Is this correct?"

"Yes ma'am. I had a fight with my girlfriend. It's not a big deal, but I wasn't around no Melanie that whole night. I don't even know her."

"When you were fighting with Ms. Jernigan, do you recall the time of evening?"

Stan looked at Melanie continuously. She noticed him when she looked up at the jury and he caught her eye. He nodded and posted a thin smile on his face. She noticed his eyes stayed on her, but let it go. She figured her nerves were working overtime that day anyway.

"No. I don't. I guess around eleven or so. She had come home from work."

"Thank you. So at the time of the rape, you were at your apartment."

Dave stood up. "Your honor. Does the defense have anything

else they can ask? We have established the same information. Mr. Shaw was at his apartment at eleven."

"You have anything else for your witness?" The judge was becoming irritated with the circular retort.

"No." She didn't know anything else. It was all up to the jury to either believe or not to believe.

Gabe walked off the witness stand and walked down to the defense table. He was worried that Mr. Mushane had something up his sleeve. He was furious that Grace didn't show up, but he really didn't blame her. He would have hung her out to dry if it was switched around.

"I would like to call Mr. Longenbecker, the landlord."

The scruffy man had on a greasy pair of jeans and a plaid short-sleeved shirt, with black Converse sneakers. He was out of place as he trudged to the front. Margaret rolled her eyes.

He was sworn in and Dave stood to ask his questions. One by one, Mr. Longenbecker answered that Gabe was at the apartment complex and that he had been fighting. But then the table turned on Gabe. "Do you remember Mr. Shaw going to his apartment after the argument in the lobby?"

"No, he didn't."

"Can you elaborate?"

"Yeah, he burned her clothes, she came back for them and they got into it right there in front of everyone. I saw her smash a hole in the wall beside his head and he called her all sorts of names. She ran out and swore it was over. She did that all the time, so I figured she'd be back. He ran out and chased her quite a ways down the road. People stood out there on the street looking at this crazy woman and this nutcase duke it out in the street in front of a phone booth. It was something, all right."

He turned to deliberately look at Gabe and then the jury. "I bet. Thank you, Mr. Longenbecker. No more questions." Dave turned back to the jury, "You now see that it is possible that in a rage, Mr. Shaw could be mistaking his whereabouts at the one o'clock hour, when Ms.Crawford was actually attacked." He proudly sat down.

Gabe looked at the jury, as each of them glared in his direction.

The only one who wasn't looking at him was Stan, or Mr. Jurney.

Margaret declined any questioning of Longenbecker. It would probably cut her throat. She was going to lose. The jury was dismissed for deliberation. They were only gone three hours before returning with a verdict.

"Madam Foreperson? Have you reached a decision on the charge of sexual assault in the second degree?"

"We have. We find the defendant, Gabriel Shaw, guilty of sexual assault in the second degree."

"And on the charge of rape in the first degree, what say you?"

"We find Mr. Shaw guilty of rape in the first degree."

Gabe's demeanor fell as he realized, his fate had been determined by a room of twelve people. He stood to his feet with shaky legs and sweaty palms. Margaret patted him on the back and said, "It'll be okay. We'll find a way."

He was cuffed and stared at the judge as he listened to the date of his sentencing. Two officers on either side shuffled him off to his cell.

The jury had an easy job that day. Stan became irritated at the outcome. He figured that the case would have lasted longer than this, at least a couple of days. His idea was ruined. How would he see her more? He thought to himself, *All that work, for this?* His teeth ground together as he wrung his hands. Sweat began to build under his arms and he suddenly had to leave for fear that the mask would begin to peel off at the sides, revealing his farce. He darted outside and the sun blaring down didn't help his situation. As his arm waved down a cab, he used the other hand to press the skin back down on his forehead and around his ears. He had to get to his apartment and figure out something else that would put him in Melanie's path, again. He stewed in front of his mirror, wondering what had gone wrong with the coffee.

Reasoning it out to himself, he talked to the face in the mirror.

"I know that had to be worse than just a seizure. How did he get out of the hospital so quickly? Why didn't he at least go into a coma? I am not going to let him get in the way anymore." He turned his head towards the wall and began to bang on the wall with his forehead. "Think, Stanley, Think!" He quickly turned and yanked the mask off, threw it in the trash and brooded over his idea being cut so incredibly short. Who would have thought that the jury would have come to a conclusion so quickly? How could they have believed that this idiot, Gabe, was guilty of something this thought out? He was appalled, because he knew Gabe didn't have much taste and even less intelligence.

Mark watched his family get out of the car, Jason included. As he met them at the door, he looked for a sign of how the case went.

"Melanie, are you okay? How did it go?" He pressed her for information.

"He's in jail. I have to admit, I don't really feel much safer, but at least he's not able to watch me anymore."

"He won't watch you, or even bother you ever again." Glenn grinned with joy that he assisted in putting Gabe Shaw in prison. He never thought that it was the wrong man. It never crossed his mind. He was so settled in the idea that someone paid for the sins against his daughter that he became blind-sighted at the true facts. The jury was ready to put someone away, as well. He knew that. He also knew that the circumstances, and his name, gave more influence in the decision made by the jury. They respected him, he was powerful and so his daughter must deserve to be granted justice. They were as blind-sighted as the rest. Someone would go to jail.

Abby looked in the refrigerator for a Coke bottle. She needed a dose of sugar and caffeine. She poured her glass and offered one to the others. They remained standing as they went into exciting, yet brief, details of the courtroom scene. Mark was completely enthralled.

"You know, Dad. I may just need to be a lawyer. Is it always exciting?" His hand patted Glenn's shoulder and they exchanged warm glances at each other.

Breaking from the look, Glenn spoke up, "No. It's mostly paperwork and research. The courts are rarely the main job. I've seen you procrastinate on papers. You might want to rethink."

The room filled with laughter. It was light and cheerful. Where was Barbara? Nobody seemed to notice until she walked through the hallway and peered into the kitchen.

"Good afternoon, everyone. I have some good news for you all."

Throwing a pamphlet, and what looked like a contract on the counter, she said, "I have found a new place to live. I know you will be glad to have me leave. But you better know, I'm not angry and I don't feel badly. I understand that I have been difficult and I'm terribly demanding. Your grandpa always told me I was expecting too much. Anyway, I will not leave without the promise that you will allow me to come visit."

Everyone remained quiet at her announcement and without saying anything, Glenn reached over and held her hand. Barbara's eyes filled with tears and she hugged him gently, and quietly whispered in his ear, "I love you *and* your family."

"Mom, we are glad that you have found a place you'll enjoy. I do promise that you are more than welcome to come over and visit."

"Just call us to make sure we're home, Barbara. I will enjoy seeing you stop by." Abby touched her other hand and they smiled.

TWO DAYS LATER

"This is the messaging service of Dr. Boone, of the Crime Scene Unit. I can't take your call so please leave a message and your number. I will get back to you ASAP. Beep."

"Um, Dr. Boone, this is Troy Garrett from the lab and I need to find some information about two chemicals that I find to be very puzzling. I have reason to believe that something may be wrong and I would like you to look into it. Give me a call or just run by when you have a minute. Thanks, uh, bye."

"He wasn't there?"

"No, but you know, I don't know why he would have the answers. We know more about chemistry than he does. I guess I just want to cover all the bases. Besides, if he will get involved, maybe he will let me assist him. I've been wanting to help solve a real crime."

"Troy, you have solved crimes."

"No, I've solved misdemeanors and dinky little mysteries, not real juicy crimes. If something weird is going on then I want to be a part of it. Why did I go to college and take all those classes in science?"

He thought about what he'd said, and then remembered the destination that the Rubidium had been shipped to. The university.

"Jan, give me a rundown on the university's recent shipments of Rubidium. Also, check for the Ethidium Bromide. That one's a curious one to find."

The computer worked quickly, showing the most recent shipment of Rubidium to the nearby college as February tenth. It showed the same date for the Ethidium Bromide, both from the same company, Erdmann Chemistry and Lab Supply, Oakland, California.

"So, should I see if Dr. Boone would let me go with him to search the school for the evidence of these elements?"

Troy was getting his hopes up as Jan looked at him and said, "There is nothing that says that school labs aren't supposed to have these specific things. You know that. Just because the labs supply them, doesn't point to any kind of foul play or whatever you're thinking."

"Jan, think about it. Maybe I've watched too many cop shows, but when was the last time blood was found in a car, not reported stolen, but a week later the owner was found missing? And, wait…when was the last time that latex had been found near the bloodstain in that same car? And, let me go on…I wonder when the last time you saw such a high amount of Rubidium in someone's system, where it didn't kill them or force a coma? Tell, me that this is all a huge coincidence? I think not!" He stood up and began to march down the hall with a sheet of paper and a heavy look of seriousness on his face. People passed him and said their greetings, but his mission was too great and he didn't hear them.

"Jan, where did Troy go?" It was Doctor Boone.

"He went to look for you. He's going to convince you about some conspiracy in the chemistry labs at the college. He thinks that he would be good at helping you crack the case."

"Why? What case? What does he think is going on?"

She explained the complete details and went deeper on the effects of each element and how it works with each substance it comes in contact with. Boone knew all of this and yet, out of kindness, obliged her thoroughness.

He lifted his finger in a point to the ceiling and then bit on his fingernail as he replied, "Well, now Jan, I can see where he is coming from. It is terribly unusual to have these findings, considering how they were used or shall I say, discovered. I'll head him off at my office. Jan, have a great day." His Old Spice lingered in the room several minutes after he had gone. She noticed it was a nice deviation from the smell of chemicals. Jan continued her work diligently.

"Dr. Boone, I found something." Nobody was in the office, so he sat himself down and waited. When Dr. Boone appeared, the older man looked at him and asked for the paper in Troy's hand.

"May I?" He read intently and then looked up with a serious demeanor. "Troy, come into my office. I think we need to look into this further." Together they sat in the glass office discussing and charting and deliberating over the facts.

Doctor Boone looked up a list of reported crimes from January to June. He read it over and over and noticed that the rape was listed in March. It had become infamous in the town. Since it was the most harsh and unusual crime the town had faced in years, he decided to pull up the details on the computer. While he read, with Troy looking over his shoulder, they concentrated intently.

Troy suddenly burst out, "Masks! There were two of them." Troy became ecstatic over the finding.

"Troy, I think we've got something to go on here. I'll go check the masks from evidence holding and you can analyze them and see if the findings coincide."

Troy read on, his heart pounding with a surge of nervous excitement. The report included the argument that left Melanie out in the park. The boyfriend's name was there but he read right over it.

He read further and found the names of the officer who handled the case and how they went about questioning. Again, the victim was questioned, but remembered little details. The boyfriend's name was mentioned once more. That time it sounded familiar to him. The first and last name, he'd seen them before. "Jason Lang. Jason Lang. Where..." He filed through his papers and read the fax from Dr. Halburk. Jason Lang! There it was. He knew it. Something was criminal and it all revolved around the Crawfords and the Lang boy. Troy vowed to find the answers.

Margaret sat with her hands over her face, not wanting to face anyone. Again, she'd lost another case. She was getting more and more to the point of hating her profession. She looked out the window and noticed her car sitting in her parking space and desired to drive away and not come back.

Her phone rang, startling her and bringing her back to reality. "Margaret Ritchey, can I help you?"

There was a brief bit of silence and then she heard a click, as if something had been turned on or off. A mechanical voice spoke, "I think you did a poor job of representing your client today. You couldn't form a shred of doubt to anyone in there. What burns me most, the case is over and I did so much to be able to sit and watch the festivities. They are over. I will make you sorry for not being capable of prolonging the case." He hung up.

"Hmmm? Gail? Can you come in here?"

"Yeah, what?"

"Did you send a phone call in here?"

"No. You were on your private line."

"Well..."

She grew shaky and her face turned pale. Gail noticed and, though she didn't want to, she helped her boss sit down. "Margaret, what is wrong with you?"

"I had a phone call. It sounded like a machine but he said horrible things. I can't figure it out. He mentioned the court case today. He was mad at me for not making it last longer. Isn't that odd? He said he'll make me sorry for not helping him."

"It could have been Gabe."

"No, he's not allowed to use the phone right now. I'm all right. I just need a cup of water."

"Hold on. If Gabe didn't call you about the case, then who would have been there to know it was over in such a short time?"

"Gail. I need a cup of water. Please? Do you mind?"

As she put the cone cup under the water dispenser, she continued, "I'm just thinking, maybe you should get a detective to check this out."

"I know protocol for this type of thing. Thank you." She snatched the water from Gail's hand. Gail took the hint as she excused herself and began her work once more.

Margaret decided to call it a day. Nothing had gone her way and she was ready to hop into the tub and take a long, hot bath and then put herself to bed.

Gail picked up the phone and called a friend of hers. "This is Gail. Hey, can you possibly do a favor for me?...I think someone may be after my boss...yes, I know how she treats people, but I don't want her to get hurt...would you mind following her and just keeping an eye on her? She got really spooked by a phone call today... Oh, thank you. Actually, come by here and get me first. Bye."

Chapter 21

Margaret reached her home looking forward to peace and quiet. She hadn't been home more than five minutes when her phone rang. She let the machine get it. She didn't hear anything, then a click, and then the voice.

"I see you. Ms. Ritchey, I see everything. I won't rest until he has died." The phone hung up and the machine rewound and announced, "You have one message."

"I've heard that before. Where? 'I won't rest until he has died'." She closed her eyes and then remembered something written on a piece of paper put on her windshield. Rummaging through her purse, she found a wadded up yellow sheet with scratchy handwriting. There was only one word she could distinguish the first time she read it; died. Now, as she looked at it, every word was legible. She took the tape out of her machine, and slid it in a zip-loc baggie along with the paper. "I won't be terrorized. You have come to the wrong person." She spoke with strength.

As she ran her bath and gathered up her hair into a bun, a soft knock broke her peaceful feeling. The deadbolts were locked and the chain was connected, and yet she was still frightened. In her robe and slippers, she grabbed her gun from her underwear drawer. Making her way slowly, she asked, "Who is it?"

"It's Gail. I've got Jeffrey Conrad here."

"Who?"

She unlocked the door and let the door open slightly. "What do you need, Gail?" Her hip leaned on the doorknob and her hand rested on her hip. She was not in the mood.

"This is Jeffrey Conrad. He's my good friend but he's also a private investigator. I called him because I was worried about the call you received."

"Gail, you shouldn't have done that. I can protect myself. If there is a nutcase out in the bushes waiting for me, then he'll have to get past my thirty-eight. Thank you but no thanks." She tried to shut the door. The door closing was stopped by the foot of the tall, slender man. He looked to be a baseball player or something. She didn't see him as the investigator type.

"No, really. I'm not interested." She tried once more to shut the door as he spoke directly to her.

"Ms. Ritchey, you need to at least give me a chance to hear what he said. If you would oblige me that much, I will leave you alone…if, and only if, I find it to be a false worry." His brilliant blue eyes captivated her and she loved the deep dimples that appeared when he smiled or said certain words. She didn't want to but she heard herself agree. "Oh, all right. Come in."

The threesome sat around the coffee table. Gail and Jeffrey shared the love seat, while Margaret sat alone in an oversized leather chair. As she looked down at her attire, she became acutely aware of the fact that she was donning a robe and her hair was pulled up in a hair clip. She rose from her seat and excused herself. Soon she entered the room in a comfortable pair of workout pants and a t-shirt.

Suddenly, looking at his face, she felt the need to tell everything. Maybe she wanted to feel safe. Maybe she wanted to know him better.

"So, tell me," Jeffrey pressed.

"I answered the phone, and at first I heard nothing and then there was a little click, like something was turned on. His voice sounded kind of like he was talking into a can."

"Did he know your name?"

"Yes, he knew my name and he said that he had been looking forward to sitting there, he used the words, 'watching the festivities.' He criticized my representation and then he said something like, 'I did so much to get there.' Something like that anyway."

"Have you had anything occur previously that would make you think this would be stalking?"

"I got this note on my windshield." She grabbed her purse and took out the baggie, which held the note and the tape.

She handed the entire thing to him and watched as his forehead crinkled as he read the cryptic sentence. He pulled the tape out and looked at her puzzled. "What's this?"

"That was left on my machine. I didn't pick up but I heard it when he left it. It happened about five minutes after I got home."

"May I?" He walked to her machine on the counter and popped in the tape. They all crowded around and listened.

When it was over, Jeffrey looked at Gail and smiled. "Well, guess I have a job, huh?"

"I really can take care of myself." Margaret tried to convince herself that she really could. Jeffrey didn't buy.

"That's nice to hear, but you know, I'm on this one. You have someone who knows your name, your phone number, your whereabouts, your case file, and what car you drive. My dear, you have a problem." She liked that he called her dear. "That's why I'm here. I'll put a tap on your phones, have surveillance on your house and *I* will follow you. Remember that anything you say on the phone needs to last a minute or longer in order for me to find out exactly where the call is coming from."

"I know all of this. Are you going to be able to see me wherever I am?"

"In public, yes. I don't think it's necessary to see inside your house if I have surveillance around the clock. Anyone who comes in or goes out will be seen."

"I'm very hesitant about this but, whatever. I need to take my bath. The water is definitely cold by now. Will you excuse me?" Her eyes were wide and her hands shook.

Gail and Jeffrey smiled shrewdly at each other as Margaret continued to act tough. She was terrified and did a horrible job trying to hide it. He knew tough exteriors and hers was not one.

As they left and got into the car, Jeffrey looked at Gail and said, "I see what you mean. She can be really hardheaded. I'm going to call Max to get over here and watch overnight and I'll have Tim start at six in the morning."

Inside, Margaret wasn't at ease. She never figured that she would be a target of terror. She hoped that the bath would soothe her and calm her nerves. It did, until she got out and got in bed and began to think again. The sentence kept going through her head.

"I won't rest until he has died." She couldn't think of anyone who might send her this or even who "he" was referring to. Was it talking about Gabe? She reached into her bedside table, grabbed the bottle of muscle relaxers and popped one in her mouth swallowing without water.

Stan wandered into his apartment after he realized the party with Margaret was over. He wouldn't bother her anymore. He had to stay under the radar and he couldn't do that with the amount of protection she had rallied up. He couldn't even get back into her house to get his camera or the bug on the phone. She was ruining his day completely. What with the end of the trial in such a swift manner and now the ability to terrorize her was put to a stop. He had to come up with something else. It was becoming fun, more like a rush. He didn't know he would find it to be a task with so much reward. If only he could get close to Melanie again. Jason was in the way and there was no way he could keep putting Rubidium in his coffee. He didn't have an easy way of explaining the diminishing amount in the chemistry lab.

His arm reached for the closet door and he sat at his desk pondering over his next move. It had to be stellar. It had to change things. He eyed the mask and became angry at the amount of time he spent becoming someone else. The case was supposed to last for days. He wondered what he should do about the mask. He decided to keep it for a memory, though he didn't know why he would want to remember Evan Jurney.

He put himself to bed. The next morning brought no more answers to his dilemma. His classes would start at eleven but he would have to work at the coffee shop until then. He would have no time to really make another move toward Melanie. He got ready and grabbed his book bag so he could go from one place to another without having to return home.

It was a miracle that he was even able to go to college. His upbringing had been so lacking. His mother made very little effort to be around and he taught himself how to read. He was responsible for getting himself to school, cooking his meals and keeping the house. When she was there she was either drunk, high or molesting him. He was her boxing bag or her toy. She didn't really want him in the first place. He knew that. She'd said it many times and made no effort to let him think differently. To manage coping with his home life, he worked hard on his grades and graduated with the top two percent. Based on his merit he was awarded a full scholarship to college. Based on his life, he was plagued with hatred and a need to be accepted. He was an unusual person to say the least. He knew that it would be hard to find friends therefore he remained a loner, dedicated to his science.

He had no other plans and figured that he would have to admire Melanie from afar. He would not be able to approach her. He would not be able to love her. He didn't know how to love her. He didn't know how to love anyone.

Dr. Boone sat at his desk with a pencil in his forefinger and thumb. He bounced it up and down as he pondered the newest findings. The case of Jason Lang's blood workup and the material found in the car had his mind running circles. "How can these two be related? The odd usage of the materials were perplexing but I find it interesting that a recent shipment of both were sent to the college around the time of the crime." He talked to himself and muddled through theories as quickly as he could talk himself out of them.

Reasoning was his specialty, but he didn't like the process of doubt that it brought too. He enjoyed the puzzles that his job brought and somehow he managed to figure them out in a timely manner. He put a call into Officer Myers.

"This is Boone with criminalistics. I would like to speak with you on a case that you worked; the rape case of Melanie Crawford. I have a feeling that there is a link between it and a case of poison with her boyfriend, as well as a missing person. Is there a time when I can meet with you?"

"Yeah, I guess I can beat it over there in about an hour. Will that work?"

"Sure. See you then. If you can, bring anything you have on the case and anything you have on Evan Jurney, the missing man."

"You got it. Bye."

The meeting took place in Boone's office, behind closed doors. Together they read reports, recalled information, stewed over ideas and came to two conclusions: someone was trying to do away with Melanie's boyfriend and the missing man had a strange connection. They couldn't come up with any more.

"You know, I don't think we're going to get anything from just sitting here. I think we need to find out where Jason got his coffees and start questioning the employees. If it was only *his* coffee that was poisoned, then it stands to reason that someone deliberately put it there." Myers was quick.

"Well, that's a great idea. Why don't we do that?" Dr. Boone rolled his eyes and picked up the phone to find out which coffee shop Jason had been frequenting.

"I got my coffee at the coffee shop on Main Street. Both times I got sick it was there. Why?" Jason probed with intrigue.

"Well, it has come to our attention that there is a possibility it was calculated. I mean that it is evident that you were a target. The amount of rubidium was extraordinarily high for coffee. The fact that it was increasing each time you had a coffee from the same shop, well, let's just say I am suspecting that you were a target, as I said."

"Who would want to hurt me? I can't think of any reason why. Do you know who put it in there?"

"No, not a clue. Myers has mentioned that you could help us a bit, though. Are you up for something like that?" Dr. Boone smiled a cautious and gentle smile, hoping it wouldn't seem like a dangerous effort. "We guarantee that you will be monitored through the entire process. It will be completely safe."

Jason's mind was running circles trying to come up with an answer. He didn't want to be frightened but he had to face the fact that he was. It never crossed his mind that the aim was pointed at him. With Melanie's rape it just seemed so unlikely that anything more could happen, to either of them. With a slight bit of fortitude he looked at Dr. Boone and Officer Myers. "Sure, I'll do it."

"Thank you. It's going to be interesting to see what we end up finding out, if anything."

"You know, it might not prove anything," Officer Myers popped in.

"But then, it could prove everything. We aren't positive that the connection between the rape, the poison, and the missing man is conclusive."

Jason's mouth dropped open as he stewed over the last statement. "What do you mean? The missing man? Who are you talking about?"

"A missing man was reported and the car that he drove was found on the interstate. There was an odd substance that was found to have Ethidium Bromide, an element that was recently purchased and shipped to the local college. The same company shipped Rubidium to the college as well. It's very suspicious that both were shipped and both were found in relation to the things that happened recently."

"When was the Ethidium used in relation to me?"

"It's Ethidium Bromide and it was found in latex as the medium for a dye. It's not really in relation to you. But we know that the same substance was found in the mask retrieved when your girlfriend was raped."

"Oh my Gosh! You're serious. Someone could want to be hurting both of us? But how does the man who's missing fit in?"

"We don't know. He may not, but there is no reason we shouldn't cover all bases. If we find out more, we might be able to find the whereabouts of Mr. Jurney."

"Is that the man?" Jason was beginning to enjoy the idea of being a crime fighter. His part would be small but it was exciting to think that he would have a part in something big.

"Yes, Evan Jurney. His office reported his not having shown up in three days. That was about two and a half weeks ago. Two nights before the report, his car was found on the side of the highway. We searched but there was no body found. The car had a weird skin-like substance and that leads us to you."

Dr. Boone had opened the case to a civilian, which was very unusual. He was not one to allow the public to know details of cases, but something told him that he wouldn't be able to figure the set of circumstances without help from outside. The connection had to be there. He knew it, he just didn't know how or why.

"Okay, Jason. Tomorrow morning you and Melanie should go to your usual coffee shop and order the exact same thing you had before. Don't drink out of the cup but make it look like you are. While you sit inside, make a mental picture of the employees and try to remember if anyone looks familiar. It may be a person who always works there and knows you, at least by face and morning ritual."

"Really, we only go there on Saturday mornings or after Melanie gets out of school. Since she's out now, do you think we should go then or will it matter?"

"Well, yeah. Whenever you usually go. Just make sure it's your predictable routine. Anyway, after you get the people in your head, come out with the coffee and bring it to the lab. We'll run it and see if there is more metal in it. I guess we're hoping in a way that there is. Oh, and make sure you get the name of the person serving you."

Jason was fired up about his assignment. As he left and got into his car, he called Melanie to tell her about the plan. He made her promise that the information would stay between the two of them. He had to make sure that he didn't jeopardize the situation.

Mark stared into the mirror flexing his muscles. He didn't have much in the way of bulk but the definition was impressive. He growled as he posed and talked to himself about how beautiful he was. "God, you made a masterpiece of me didn't you."

It hit him. He said it. He attributed his form to God. "Whoa. I've got to get a grip. I'm starting to believe in something I don't believe in."

"Mark, you got a minute?" It was his mother. He grabbed a t-shirt and put it over his neck sliding his arms into the sleeves. "Yeah, just a second. Let me get some pants on. I'm changing." He heard himself murmur, "Boy am I changing." What was happening to him?

He opened the door and strangely stepped aside inviting her into his forbidden cove. She put her hand on his cheek and patted it with a sensitivity that understood his need to be solitary. He was going through the years and definitely going through the motions. She relished the moments he enjoyed her company. They were few, but precious to her.

"I just came to see how things are going." She eyed the room and noticed several posters of music bands she'd never heard of and then to her surprise, she saw a picture of the family in a brown frame next to his computer terminal. She'd been in there before but never noticed it. How could she not notice it? It was the only thing that looked familiar. She guessed it to be a recent addition to his room and her heart smiled while she thanked God for being so faithful.

"I'm doing all right. I've got to get my truck lights fixed today. I think the bulb is out. I'm hoping it's not a short in the wiring."

"Oh, that's nice." She was still occupied by the curiousness of the family picture. "Mark, have you had that there all the time?"

"What?" His eyes looked around for anything that would prompt the question.

"The picture of the family? Have you always had it in here?"

"No, well yeah. I had it here but it was in the drawer. After all the stuff we've been through, I just wanted to remember how much we stand together when things get bad. That sounds so lame, huh?" He rolled his eyes and his cheeks puffed slightly as he smiled.

"No, I think it's wonderful."

"Yeah, your son is going soft. Just don't tell anyone." He cast a huge grin at her and wanted to go hug her, but that would be too much.

"Honey, you are really a great son. I hope you know that."

"Yeah, I know." He laughed with a smirk. "Mom, I'm glad you

came in. I need to talk to you about something fairly important."

"Okay. What?" She was overwhelmed at the calm in the room and how honest they were being with each other. There were no walls it seemed.

"God."

"Mark, I'd say that's much more than fairly important. Go ahead. I'm listening." She was anxious to have a conversation with her son and to talk about the Lord made her insides jump for joy.

"I know what you believe. I know you taught me the stuff when I was a kid. But, lately, I've been thinking. Somewhere along the line, I decided that it was all just a bunch of religious junk that someone duped you and whole bunch of others into believing. I guess I stopped believing what you taught me. Do you know what I'm saying?"

"No. Not really. Keep going." She was getting confused yet remained composed so as not to push him.

"What's the reason you believe there's a God? I just want some proof."

He sat in his rolling desk chair and swiveled from side to side with nervousness. He hadn't held a decent conversation with his mother in years. He was too cool and too teenager for her. It didn't seem normal to chat with the mom. This was new and he was enjoying it.

Without hesitation, she spoke. "I know that there is a God because I know that we couldn't have faced all that we have without His power and grace. It's not something I question because I know that He is the only thing in my life that allows me to have the freedom of letting Him have my problems. He is also the Father of Jesus. I know Jesus died a horrible death because He loved me, little me. He died, but he's also the only one who has ever risen from the dead. No other religion can claim that their God has done that. It seems impossible not to believe."

"Yeah, I know all that. What makes me wonder is why He allows bad things and then still expects us to worship Him as usual? Why would anyone have to suffer if He loves us so much?"

"He's not the one responsible for our pain. He allows it so that we will put our faith in him and let Him handle things. We can't bear everything on our own. He knows that, but we do have the choice in whether we will be under His umbrella. It still rains, but the umbrella keeps us a little drier than if we didn't have it. If we didn't have it, or Him, we'd be a lot more wet and searching for a place to run. Others run, but they find things that only satisfy for a while. He satisfies eternally."

"The umbrella. Do you think that the umbrella was on Melanie when she was raped?" His voice gave a tone of discomfort leading into anger.

"Mark, I know that it's hard to understand why someone like your sister would be hurt so badly. I don't understand the reason either. We may not know. Someone sick and depraved was under Satan's hand and I can't explain why it was aimed at your sister. It shouldn't happen to anyone, but I honestly think that if it weren't for the circumstances that we have been dealt, you and I wouldn't be having this conversation." Her voice was so soft and her eyes became watery.

"I know you're right. I have been thinking that all this time. I just needed to hear it. God does exist. I believe and I've been fighting it because I didn't want to understand that kind of love. It's unfathomable, but I think I feel that way about you and Dad and Mel."

"Mark, I love you. You are so wise and I know that sometimes the smartest people are the hardest to convince. I want to pray with you when you are ready. I won't push you."

"I can pray right now. I'm not afraid."

Abby's hand reached over and held Mark's. They looked at each other and leaned in putting their foreheads together. She prayed aloud and then Mark prayed. His prayer was the most humble and honest. He admitted to his doubts and fears and asked for forgiveness for his faults and deliberate sins. His voice cracked as he asked Jesus to become a part of his heart. He allowed the Holy Spirit to intervene and the words that he couldn't voice went straight to the Father. He felt a peace and a new calm. Together, he cried with Abby. The day she'd waited for was here and it was better than she'd ever anticipated.

"I love you, Mom." He hugged her for a long time.

"Margaret, I was told you are under surveillance. What do they think you're into?" Glenn had a tone of sarcasm as he spoke over the phone.

"Well, Glenn, I am not into anything. Thank you for the confidence. No, I've got some freak calling my home and office and a few weeks ago I received a note on my car. How is it that surveillance of me becomes public knowledge. Doesn't that defeat the purpose?"

"I know people. I'm not just public and you know I won't say anything. I'm sorry about it. What are the calls about?"

"I don't have the foggiest. The note said he wouldn't rest until he died."

"Until he died? Who died?"

"I don't know. The phone calls were weirder than that. The call at the office was about the case against Gabe Shaw. He was angry with me for how short it was. I thought that was funky and then when I got home I got a call. Same person I assume, and he said he could see me and knew where I was and again, he wouldn't rest until he died."

"I wonder who *he* was referring to. You've never heard the voice before?"

"No, that was something else. Before he would talk, I would hear silence and then a click like something turned on. Then the voice sounded like a machine. No way for me to recognize it." She pursed her lips wondering why he was so concerned. He didn't ever like her, and she had no real reason to like him either. He was a show off in the courtroom and he had a following that she envied in secret. She was a court appointed attorney who didn't win cases, except in a blue moon.

"What do you want, Glenn?"

"Well, I want to know if I can help you in any way. I know the case the other day was rough and I can't help but think that you were bitter over it, or me."

"Yeah, well, we can just chalk it up to another great loss in the annals of Margaret Ritchey. I'm used to it, but right now, I don't need it rubbed in. I've got a lot going on and to say I'm scared is an understatement."

"I'm not rubbing it in. I know what you were up against and I want to apologize for the, well, everything. I've given you some grief since law school and you never asked for it." She was shocked at his words. He was always so cocky and self-absorbed. She'd never seen the warm side of him and it was a nice change.

"Glenn, thank you. I appreciate your call. I'll let you go back to your big office work." She almost put the phone down but heard his voice speaking.

"Marg, I think you need to tell me more about the calls. I'm interested."

"Are you going to charge me hourly? 'Cause you know I can't afford you."

He laughed and said, "No. I am, however, very concerned. I think it's odd that he did it after the court case. I also find it strange that he was angry that it was over so soon. Do you think that he was possibly in the courtroom, watching, maybe?"

She was puzzled by his interest but the questions were already formed in her mind as well. If she had Glenn on her side, there was some safety in knowing that. "Glenn, I've thought about that too. It's making me rehash everything he said. He said he wanted to watch the show. I don't know what he meant by that but I am starting to become convinced that whoever it is, he saw the case. It wasn't televised or even covered by the press so…"

"It was like a concert in there. So many people came to watch that it would be impossible to find them all and go that route. I do think that it would be to your advantage to have another incident occur."

"Yeah, but there isn't any way that will happen. I have a private eye watching my home and office and the phones are tapped. If he has known my whereabouts all along, then he would know that there is someone looking out for me. He won't make any moves. How do you think we should find out who it is? Ask if anyone knows someone who speaks like a machine and wants someone dead?"

"I don't know. Marg, how about I talk to the PI and see if I can get a little more involved? The fact that this weirdo said he wanted to see the show, and the case involved my daughter…"

Margaret broke in with a bit of sensitivity in her voice. He'd never heard this side of her. She was scared and touchy. Everything was too much for her then. "I know. I appreciate it. I'll get you his number. His name is Jeffrey Conrad."

"Oh, he's good. I know him personally. I've got the number. Let me get in touch with him and we need to all meet. Call you later?"

"Sure, I'll be here all day." They hung up. Glenn hurriedly called Jeffrey and Margaret pretended to work under the duress. She wondered why she was even at the office. It crossed her mind that she felt safer there, but she didn't. She felt as if eyes were on her, even if they were the surveillance of the other investigator. It made her crazy.

Not long had she hung up from the call with Glenn when the phone rang again. She was frozen for a minute then grabbed the receiver. It was Glenn. "Meet us at the coffee shop on Main Street. Three this afternoon."

"Okay. See you then."

She was truly grateful to Glenn. For the first time he was interested in something important. He usually dealt with business law or high profile cases. Since it was his daughter, the peons seemed a little more worthy of his valuable time. She understood the change of his heart. It was personal this time. She became puzzled at his pressing of information since the case was over and the jury found Gabe guilty.

The tires were still on the wheels as the white sedan was hoisted up into the air of the Crime Scene Investigation garage. Two men in blue coveralls with the letters CSU on their backs wandered around and looked up under the auto. The car could help give clues as to the site of its owner. They put their hands on the tires and with a metal tool scraped off red dried dirt. The dirt was dropped into a small glass vial and put aside. They made a model of the tire tread and looked around the base of the car for any other clues they might have missed before.

"Look at this. What do you think?"

"I think it's got to be hair and blood. There isn't anymore anywhere. Maybe it's from a dead animal on the road. Let's analyze it."

The two went up to the lab with their findings and handed the hair sample to the Jan, the technician. "Check this out. Let us know if it's anything that will give us a lead."

She took it and placed it on a glass film, covered it and slid it into the microscope. As she looked at it, she noticed the roots were still in tact and skin was holding on. It wasn't a lot to go by but she was sure it had been pulled out with force. She continued to analyze the hairs.

"I have something here. It's human hair."

They all glanced at each other as their hopes began to rise and the adrenaline pumped harder. Was it Evan Jurney's? The three ran to the room next door and waited as Troy checked for a DNA match. It matched. Now they had to find out what kind of dirt was on the tire and where it came from.

College students and businessmen crowded the coffee shop. Seats were scarce. Glenn sat down with Jeffrey Conrad at the only table with three chairs available. It sat close to the window allowing the sun to beat on them with intensity as they waited for Margaret to enter.

The door jingled when someone entered or exited. Margaret made her entrance as a man pushed the door to go out. She meandered over to the table and sat down smiling with a look of frantic wonder. "So, am I out of the picture, yet?"

"No, not yet. You haven't received any calls today, have you?" Jeffrey asked her knowing the answer.

"No, thanks to you. I don't know what we will accomplish here.

Why are we meeting?"

"We are going to try to use you as bait." Glenn looked serious and then grinned. Stan kept his eyes on them, listening to their every word. He could hear them clearly, in spite of the bustling noises around him. It was as if he had an ear just for their voices. Whatever they were planning, he would know about and it wouldn't work in their favor. He would make sure of that.

"No, you're not. I'm not bait for anyone. I don't know that I even *want* to find out who is doing this. Get another plan, guys."

"Marg, you have to trust us. It's not going to be all that dangerous. All we want to do is act as if we're taking the surveillance off and debugging the phone lines. If he thinks you're back to regular life, he may return to his games. All the time we will know what's going on."

"How do you know he won't know you know?" She questioned him worried and disturbed.

"Just trust us. It's just us. We're taking care of the details and you just resume your regimen." Jeffrey tried to reassure her but knew that her apprehension might end up backfiring on the whole deal.

"I don't like this, but I will do it anyway. You promise to back me up. You can't leave me hanging. I'll never forgive you, either of you." She stared straight at them, finger pointing at both men and eyes wild with distress.

The door jingled once more and Glenn looked surprised at the couple. "Melanie, baby. What are you doing? Hi Jason."

"Daddy, hi. We didn't expect to see you here."

"Yeah, we're working on something. This is my daughter and her boyfriend, Jason." He had a proud look on his face as he held Melanie's small hand in his.

"I can't help but think it's odd to see the two of you working on something, together." Her brow crinkled and her eyes slimmed looking Margaret's direction. She remembered her from the previous times and knew she was rude and harsh.

"Margaret had a problem after the court scene the other day. Since it's over, we've decided to work to resolve it along with the help of

Mr. Conrad, here." He motioned to Jeffrey.

"Working on what? What happened?" Melanie was interested. The court case had rattled her but to know that a problem happened afterwards, it made her anxious. Why was her dad getting involved?

"Did you come in for coffee? You seem to be a glutton for punishment, Jason." Glenn laughed. "What are you doing here?"

"We're working on something too," Jason whispered.

"Oh, and that would be?" Glenn whispered back.

"It's for the police and the crime lab. I'll tell you about it later, okay, Dad."

Glenn's forehead creased as he became worried. He nodded and said, "See you at home, then." They turned to walk away and he grabbed her hand again. "Baby, don't do anything crazy. Be careful." She smiled and nodded, moved by his statement of care and concern.

As Melanie approached the counter, Jason stood behind her with his hand resting on her shoulders. The place was so busy since the summer break had begun. Customers bustled and bumped into each other, holding hot coffee with great care. Employees scurried behind the counter to take orders and create concoctions. When she stood there long enough, a man, about thirty, stood behind the cash register and echoed her order to the man behind him. Jason then ordered and the man echoed again.

The man creating delicious drinks in the back stopped and turned around. He'd been occupied by the other orders but when he heard her voice, he had to see her again. The last time he saw her, she was sitting in a wooden pew in the courtroom, watching the wrong man pay for a crime he didn't commit. Her voice stood out so easily. He had it engrained on his memory and there was no mistaking it. It was distinct and perfect. It was melodic and beautiful.

Jason was standing right next to her. He sneered and mumbled several remarks as he looked down at the ground. They stepped to the side and waited for their orders to come up. Jason stared at the man fixing his cup of coffee. He didn't notice anything strange, nothing different being put into the cup. It was just as it had been the other times when he hadn't gotten sick. The order was up and as

Stan handed the cups over, his eyes bore a hole through Jason. Jason did notice that. The nametag said Stan. That was all it said. He didn't know any more than that. He did remember seeing him the other times they had been in the shop. But nothing about him ever stood out and he surely didn't have any bad feelings. Jason made a great point of being cordial. He wondered about the look he had just received. Jason took the cups, handing one to Melanie and then eyed Stan looking at them. The look changed from a scowl to a friendly, warm smile. That was odd.

Since there were no seats available Jason and Melanie left the shop and headed straight for the lab.

Stan stood statuesque and kept them under observation until he could no longer see them. He thought to himself, *That was a crazy move, Stan. You are going to foul this up if you aren't careful. I just get so mad thinking about Jason and his perfect world. She doesn't know him. He certainly doesn't know her.* He continued to make drinks as he mulled over another way to get to Melanie. He knew if he were to get close enough, he would have to silence her completely. She couldn't know who he was.

Chapter 22

It was discovered that the dirt came from the country roads that were about thirty miles out of town. It was outlandish that Mr. Jurney would have been driving that direction when his home and office were both on the opposite end of the town. There was no reason anyone could give for the dirt being on the tires. His life was a complete schedule. He would wake up, get dressed in his business suits, go to the donut shop at the end of his street and head for work. It was predictable the time he would arrive, promptly at 7:57 a.m. He worked till lunch at one and would usually grab a sandwich in the cafeteria downstairs. He worked hard until six and then left. No one knew him to go out or socialize much. He didn't even carry on much conversation while at the office. He was friendly and cordial but not much of a talker. He had a very good rapport with one of the cute little secretaries on the third floor. It was she who noticed that he had been absent for one week. She asked his supervisor and was informed that no one had heard from him. Being that he was a terribly responsible person, it became cause for alarm. However, it took so long to notice because he stayed so low-key.

There was still no sign of him. Authorities looked and looked, in all the wrong places. They looked in the wrong direction. When the dirt was identified as being from the country, it took the law to a new search. As they scoured roads of gravel and red parched dirt, they noticed several different tire markings on the roads. Some looked like tractor tires, others like old model automobiles with worn treads. But one track on a slim patch of road hidden between high cornrows stood out. It went on forever, it seemed. No one had any idea that the road would run so far into the country. In a clearing of brush and weeds, they spotted a large mound of something.

"I see a white dress shirt covered in mud. Looks like some nice suit pants and a tie too. Think we got our guy?" He covered his nose with his entire arm and his eyes watered from the horrendous odor that emitted from the corpse. "Oh man, what a smell! It never gets easier." The officer sauntered up to the mass on the dirt and leaned over reaching into his pocket. He came up with a dollar in change but no wallet. "Well, no wallet to be found. Guess we'll have to identify him when we get back. Still, I bet it's him." Four men wandered up with a black bag and wrestled to get the body inside.

At the morgue, Dr. Boone suited up in a blue lab coat, set up his tools on the metal tray and awaited the arrival of the mystery dead man. It wasn't much of a mystery; it had to be Evan Jurney. The body rolled in on a gurney and Dr. Boone unzipped the bag. The stench had become worse on the way home, but Dr. Boone was so used to it he didn't even wince. After an hour, the doctor came out with news that wasn't alarming.

"Mr. Evan Jurney has been found. He has a stab wound to his heart from the back under the ribs. It was punctured and then twisted out. He died from a heart attack, but this had to be one painful heart attack. The knife was serrated, kind of like a hunting knife or bread knife. It was larger than a kitchen steak knife. The striations were far apart. One thing I did come across was a gooey substance in his nostrils and his ear cavities. There was a little in his teeth as well. It looks like the same stuff we found in his car. I don't know what is going on but I think someone is playing a game and Troy, it is somehow in connection with the Crawford case and Jason Lang's seizures. Where would you start from here? Think hard, because this is education for you. You might be the one to crack this case wide open."

He smiled at Troy with a hint of pride. Troy was a great scientist and a huge asset to the team. He was open to anything. Jan was more subdued and clear thinking. She didn't seem to be the kind that would jump out on a ledge to find out what the truth was. It was all science and facts to her. Instinct and danger just weren't her thing.

Jan looked at the two of them and wondered what they were talking about. She became a bit amused and even envious as she realized that they knew something big and she was out of the loop. "What's going on?"

"Well, Troy here showed me a couple of things that prompted us to look deeper into the Melanie Crawford rape case when her boyfriend Jason Lang was found with a gross amount of Rubidium in his system."

"Yeah, so? What's that got to do with the dead guy?"

"Mr. Jurney had a substance on his skin…"

"With Ethidium Bromide. I know. But, are you really thinking the three are linked? Think of the odds. What would the connection be? Of course I see the rape and the poison, but the murder? How is this man in any way related to them?" Troy was bubbling with excitement as he interjected his theory.

"Maybe not directly, but indirectly. He could have gotten in the way, perhaps. See Jan, the mask that was found at the rape site was made out of the same substance as that which was found in the car, only a lot thicker and heavier. Both contained Ethidium Bromide, a dye used in DNA gels. It's uncommon to use for latex but I can see why it would work. Both are gels, why not use it to dye something, such as a mask?"

"The Lang boy?" She was so doubtful. He rolled his eyes.

"The coffee that he remembered he had both times he became ill was tainted with Rubidium. Who would know that coffee contains trace amounts of Rubidium without doing research? Who could figure out a way for it to seem unlikely that it was poison, and not just bad coffee? But, think, if it was bad coffee why were there not more episodes of sick people? Only Jason? That's too much of a coincidence."

"I agree, but where would all of the elements have come from?" She stopped herself and realized the answer had been discovered earlier, "The university had a shipment of both from Eerdman's in March. The same month as the rape." She was getting it. Boone smiled as his team became a team and solved things together.

"Dr. Boone, we go to the university." Troy became more and more elated as the excitement grew. Suddenly there were obvious clues and the three people he worked closest with were all together.

Melanie and Jason walked into the crime lab just as the three science sleuths were walking out.

Dr. Boone stopped them and placed his hand on Jason's shoulder as they nearly passed by each other. "Mr. Lang, how are you? Do you have anything for us?"

"Yes, where do we take this sample of coffee?" Melanie spoke up with a sense of determination. The three sleuths wondered if she was genuinely excited about being there or if she was just anxious to get in and get out, most likely the latter.

"It's down the hall, take a right and then the first door on the left. A gal named Rhoda, tall, about forty-five is in there and she can do the analysis. You can wait if you'd like, the lounge is directly across from the lab. I'll be in later and I'll be anxious to see if the results give us something else to go on."

"Something else? You have something?" Jason was intrigued.

Troy interjected for Dr. Boone, "Well, let's just say we have a hunch and it's unanimous."

"Okay, we'll wait. Thanks and good luck on that hunch." Melanie and Jason walked toward the lab and finally found Rhoda. She was easy to pick out. They introduced themselves and she nodded to acknowledge her familiarity of the case. She took the coffee cups, which had now become cold and the white froth had turned to a dull film covering the top of the cup. As she pointed to the lounge, she began her testing. It was a top priority, according to Dr. Boone. Rhoda knew her way around and could perform the most difficult scientific experiments with ease as well as speed. Jason and Melanie talked small talk as they awaited the outcome. It had been nearly an hour when Rhoda motioned through the glass that she had the results. They stood and gathered each other's hand and trekked into the glass room.

"We have some good and some bad. Which do you want first?"

"The bad," Jason said as he looked at Melanie and shrugged. Either way, he would hear the news.

"Okay. The bad news is that there isn't any Rubidium in this specimen. The good news is that there isn't any Rubidium in this specimen. You would have been safe to drink it. I'm sorry that I couldn't help you more. If there had been any, I would have seen it, but the coffee was clean. You weren't the target today." Rhoda smiled and handed the coffee cups back to Jason and Melanie. "If you heat it in the microwave, you could probably drink it. It won't taste the same, though." She laughed at her joke and turned away lifting a slide into the air and checking its contents. The couple took the cue and left, throwing the cups into the trash.

"So, either the incidents were a fluke, or someone is playing a game with my life. Is it possible that the person who put it in my drink knows we are searching for answers?" Jason thought out loud while they drove back to her home. The day didn't go the way they had hoped, although, it was nice to know that no one was trying to kill Jason that day.

Glenn sat in the kitchen on a wrought iron barstool with his feet propped up on the rail of the stool beside him. He had a discontented appearance. Melanie kissed him on the cheek and he patted her on the back. He was deep in thought and didn't appear to want to be bothered.

"Daddy, you good?" she asked with concern.

"Yeah, it's just been a long day. I'm afraid that when I saw you today at the coffee shop that I left out a few details."

"That's fine. I understand. Your work doesn't concern me."

"Yes it does. This time, I believe it really does. Margaret received a note on her car a couple of days before the trial. It said, 'I won't rest until he dies.' She thought that was strange but ignored it. Then, the day of the trial, she received a call at her office that made the point of letting her know he was at the courthouse to quote 'watch the show.' And he was terribly angry that it didn't last longer than it did. She got rattled but dismissed it again. Then, she went home and received another call. The same character, we assume, said he could see her and wouldn't rest until he dies."

"Did you get who's doing that?"

"No, we have nothing to go on. She can't identify the voice because when she picks up she hears a click and then the voice sounds like it's…"

Melanie broke in with fear in her eyes. "A machine. Daddy, do you think it's the same person who called me and left the messages? Oh my gosh, if it is, then Gabe Shaw went to jail for something he didn't do. It's my fault. Daddy, what do we do? How can we get him now? Is the rapist still out there?"

She began to let her composure escape as terror ran through her body. She stood as if she were a mannequin, unable to move or talk. Her voice got weak and raspy. As Jason led her to the chair, a million thoughts came to his mind. Gabe Shaw didn't do it. Someone who was at the courthouse knew the schedule, knew the movements of the attorney, and came specifically for that trial; the trial that played games with people's lives.

"Glenn, do you have any leads on who this freak is?"

"Jason, I don't even know if it's *about* Melanie. I don't have proof but I just have this instinctive fatherly thing going on in my head. Mothers have their intuition but so do fathers. Keep her calm. By the way, your project, what was it?"

"The coffee that I had been drinking was found to have large amounts of Rubidium. You knew that, but the lab was concerned because it was so much that apparently, more than just seizures and a short stay in the hospital should have taken place. They said I'm lucky to be alive. We got coffee just like we normally do, but it wasn't conclusive to anything, except that we could drink it without dying."

"So, we have dead ends, here. What is going on in this place?" Glenn's tone ran louder and he became angrier as he thought. "I think that something has to break. Who is your contact at the crime lab, who have you been speaking with?"

"Dr. Boone."

"Well, I'm going to find out what ways we could assist in this. If someone is trying to poison you, stalks the defendant's attorney, and watched someone go to prison for something he didn't do, then I'm willing to bet that this isn't the end of it. He may know that the clues could begin pointing to him, so he may lay low, but I doubt this guy would cower like that. He seems to thrive on devouring the comfort and safety of lives."

"What do you think we should do? I can give you Dr. Boone's office number. But you know, they, he and a couple of techs, were leaving because they said they came upon something really good."

"Hmmm. I wonder how good." Glenn took the number and dialed. The machine in his office picked up so Glenn talked to it."

"We'll see what happens. Jason, can you stay with her? Abby went upstairs to find something and she should be getting back down here soon. We'll have supper in about an hour. Just try to make Melanie feel safe. If she needs to lay down, take her to the sofa and sit with her."

"No Dad, I'm fine. I was shocked at first, but I am fine. I know you are going to do everything you can to put an end to this nightmare."

Stan picked up a picture hidden under clothes in the dresser drawer. As he counted the people in it, which amounted to three, he put his finger on each one. His finger covered one small boy, leaving a slightly older boy and a woman. It was a nice picture but he thought several times about throwing it away. Memories were unnecessary in life. Laying it on top of the dresser next to an old lamp without a shade, he walked into the closet and sat at his mirror. He eyed the masks that hung on the wall. They didn't seem to matter anymore. He knew that somehow, the trick was up and his time would be short. He had nothing else to do but wait. They would find him. He watched them as much as he could, even giving up sleep. His voyeurism was not out of love, or hate, but the compulsion to be someone else for once.

Any anger he had toward Jason, Melanie or Margaret was slowly disappearing while his life was quickly turning into a cat and mouse chase. He wouldn't go down without a fight. He couldn't. His mind had been blown long before he ever saw Melanie and Jason together.

He looked for them and when he found them, his jealousy became strong, stronger than he imagined it could be. He didn't know he would be capable of the acts that he had committed, but after one, the next didn't seem as difficult. He'd crossed the barrier of grief and plunged headfirst into abhorrence. What he had was nothing. His brains had given him an identity with teachers and professors, but no one appeared to know who Stan really was. He was a hurting soul searching for a need to be met. He never knew more than pain. Life dealt him nothing in his life that he could call a gain. That's where Jason and he were so different. Jason got out, even if he didn't know it, he had escaped. All Stan really desired was to know Jason, but the time came when he resented the life he never had.

His eyes closed as he remembered scenes of his past. The woman would hold out her arms and push needles into scars from needles before. She would cry as she wondered why she was so pathetic. Her eyes would glance at the boy in the corner. He had been sent to sit there for the past seven hours as she slept on the couch in an alcoholic stupor. If he needed to relieve himself, he had to do it there. He knew he would be punished for that, as well as just being a burden to her. The television played continuously at an annoyingly high volume. Game shows and soap operas occupied the screen all day. He was very bright, but she didn't know how much. She called him names and threw beer cans at him, just because he was there. His eyes learned not to tear up when she came at him with that glazed that glazed look of hers. He knew what would happen next. The bedroom door was torn off the hinges and leaned on the wall outside his room. She did that specifically so she could keep an eye on him. Though he never understood why, since he was more of an encumbrance than a son. He was told to go lay down and she would come in several minutes later and tell him how much she hated having to do what she was doing but he had to learn his lesson. He didn't ever know what lesson that was. She was rough and hateful and made him hurt all over. She would leave as soon as she was done and he would be told to go to bed, she had things to do. Of course she did, she had to toss a few more beers down her throat and sniff something into her red nostrils. She would once again fall asleep on the couch.

One day, she didn't wake up. He covered her with a blanket and left for good. He didn't look back at the shanty house he had to refer to as home. Following the road to nowhere, he wondered where he would end up. He was allowed to live under the care of a nice man who said he'd watch over him, if he would work after school. This same helpful man set him to work as soon as he could. Money was not great and the job was even worse as the man who appeared to be an angel at first, turned into a devil. As he was pimped to anyone and everyone, it didn't seem much like he'd ever left home. He was twelve then. His grades remained excellent and a teacher in his last year of high school assisted in getting him a scholarship to college. He kept the picture in his bag and he held it tightly. As he worked hard to find the other boy in the picture, his efforts ran on for years. The hard work paid off as he finally figured out where the boy had grown up. Now, he was beginning college in a town hundreds of miles from where Stan was. Stan's scholarships allowed him the opportunity to go to the same town. He finally came face to face with his little brother. The world was so different for the two and as quickly as his memory brought back the feelings of excitement to find his long lost brother, they just as quickly turned to rage and antipathy.

Stan worked his mind back to reality slamming his hand into the closet wall, causing a hole in the sheetrock. Stan created a life for himself in spite of his childhood. He watched Jason and then it became apparent that Melanie would be in the way as well. He naturally fell for her beautiful appearance but also loathed her for it. He knew that no one was that pure, that good, that beautiful. Something had to be shown to Jason, and he knew he could be the one to show him. He watched their schedule and patterns. He knew when they were at the coffee shop and soon took a job there. He could watch them. It was perfect. They would be none the wiser.

"If Margaret had done her job, that trial could have gone on for days. I could have looked at Melanie's eyes and she would soon see mine. They would burn into her brain and she wouldn't be able to see anything else. Margaret, you are the worst lawyer I have ever witnessed. You just handed Mr. Shaw over to the jury on a platter. We believed he did it because you didn't prove he didn't." He talked out loud to himself in the mirror. Tears began to well in the corner of his eyes, but he remembered he wasn't aloud to cry. He wanted to so badly but he was a man, had to be a man.

His voice got distant and fragile and his eyes glazed over as he became trance-like. "Jason, I wanted to be like you. No one ever wanted to be like me." He put his fingernails into his cheeks and scraped them down his face, leaving marks that resembled jail bars.

His heart gave up trying to get away. He gave into the resolution that someone would be tearing down his door to take him off. He wouldn't fight them. He didn't see any reason to fight. It would happen, the clues were there and since he'd made a few mistakes along the way, he was sure to be caught.

Chapter 23

Dr. Boone introduced himself to the science professor, Dr. Monroe. They wiped the sweat that built up between their hands as they shook respectfully. Dr. Monroe invited the team in and allowed them to search for any signs of mishandling of chemicals and elements. Officer Myers had been contacted and was expected to show up anytime. They found nothing on the surface.

"Dr. Monroe, I know this is quite bothersome for you, and I do hope you accept my apologies. We are investigating a few crimes that have recently occurred. The reason we have been led here is that these particular cases involve Rubidium and Ethidium Bromide. We checked the specific companies who ship these elements and it appears that a shipment of both were sent in early March."

"You can't think that I have anything..."

"No, sir, we just need to see the shipments and find out how much of each has been used, to rule out any possibility they came from your lab."

"Oh, I can take you to the cabinet where we keep them. I can assure you that nothing out of the ordinary has come from any of my students. They are diligent students and have a tremendous respect for science. I know that science isn't the most exciting topic to everyone, but my classes are very studious. Most of them put in large amounts of hours in this very lab."

"Do you allow them to come and go as they please? Are they able to have access to everything even if you are away?"

"Not usually. Only on rare occasions, such as exam studying, experiments, things like that. I'm usually around to check in on them, in case they need assistance."

"The cabinet please?" Dr. Boone requested with a smile. Officer Myers showed up and spoke loudly, "So, what'd you find?"

As he bent down and opened the glass cabinet, Boone looked back over his shoulder at the garish display of behavior from the policeman. The cabinet had been locked, which was interesting to Troy.

"Do you keep this cabinet closed and locked at all times?"

"No, when students are working, I allow it to be accessible to them. They are all bright enough to use anything in there without causing an explosion." He chuckled at his own joke. No one else did. He shrugged and asked, "So, what exactly are you looking for?"

Dr. Boone kneeled down with one knee flat to the tile floor. His hands and eyes grazed over the names from the periodic table. He knew the majority of them and what they were capable of. There was a steady stream of names and the amounts of each compartment seemed to be equal. There didn't appear to be any missing. He didn't accept that. He pulled the tray that held the Ethidium Bromide. The element had been arranged to look as if there were still the same amount as the rest.

However, when observed from the back, there were three vials missing. The same had been done to the Rubidium. Boone's demeanor became curious as he looked over his shoulder at the professor.

"Can you account for the whereabouts of the missing pieces here?"

"No, I can't. We have done nothing this whole semester that require the use of either. I used it last semester and when we depleted the resource, I ordered more for the next fall semester. I have absolutely no idea where it would have gone."

"Well, my gloves left no fingerprints, so I am assuming that whoever used these, left their fingerprints. Do you mind?" he asked without the slightest bit of worrying if Dr. Monroe minded or not.

Troy stepped forward and sprinkled feathery bits of powder with what resembled a large make-up brush. As it dusted the area and clung to the oils of skin, it gave way for the fingerprints to be seen clearly. He took out a piece of paper that had an adhesive backing and laid it on the prints. It lifted them right off and they held perfectly onto the paper.

"Well, Dr. Monroe, it appears that as smart as your students are, they didn't think to use gloves, like I did. We'll take these prints back to the lab and have them run through our database and be able to identify our suspect. Do you have any input on this? Anyone you remember being in here alone or having complete control over the cabinet at one point? Think, because I think you might have it in your memory, but it's hiding."

"It's a long shot, because he's a wonderful person. A little on the brainy weird side, if you can believe that of a science nerd." He chuckled at his own joke once more and the others remained stiff. He ignored their lack of humor. "Anyway, I allowed him to do a Saturday study session in here right before finals. That's the only time I haven't been in the room. Of course, I guess that anyone could have just taken them and put them in their book bags without being noticed. I figure I need to be more cautious of my lab contents, huh?"

"Yes, that might help. Who is the one you're referring to? I need a name, possibly an address if you can get it."

"His name is Stan, Stan Weber. He lives in the apartments over near the stadium. I don't know the number, but really, I think that's a long shot. I'll go on record as not believing he could do anything criminal. He is so quiet and calm. He's here on a full scholarship. His mother died when he was twelve, but he made it anyway. I think he's got potential to be the next Pulitzer winner."

With a sense of disinterest, Dr. Boone began to exit the room with his team of detectives. "Yeah, the smart seem to know how to fool you and you never know it. Have a nice day, and thank you for your cooperation."

In the hallway, students passed without any cares. The most important thing to the students was to get to class on time. The most important thing for the crime bevy was to head straight to the lab and see whose fingerprints these would turn out to be. With any luck it would be the guy.

"Hi, Dr. Boone. This is Glenn Crawford. I'm calling in reference to many things. First of all, Jason Lang is very dear to us and I understand you have been working with him to find out why he got so sick recently. The second thing is that I am convinced that whoever has been doing this to Jason may be the one who raped my daughter in March and is now stalking the attorney who defended the man who went down for her rape. He's leaving notes and referring to the court case as if he had been there, and he also has repeated that he will not rest until he dies. I don't know exactly what that means or who 'he' is referring to, but I just needed to find out from your end what we can do to identify this guy and get rid of him. My number is 555-8307. Please call me as soon as you can."

"So, Mr. Crawford is putting two and two together, also. I guess our hunches are looking solid. Any match yet?"

"It's about loaded, so just a few seconds and we'll know who has been playing with things he ought not to be. Man, this is what I got into this field for. I am so psyched." Troy was over-exuberant but no one dared call him on it. His excitement was perfectly acceptable since it looked as if the answers were about to come to a head. Even Jan sat with a twinge of nervous excitement.

The screen showed several different stages of the ID development and then a flash across the screen read, "Match."

Dr. Boone spoke with authority and weight. "Stanley Weber. We've got you."

Chapter 24

Glenn picked up the phone, listened and then put the phone down. He sat with a heavy demeanor and then jumped up off the couch. "Abby, they think they've got the guy. Well, they don't have him, but they think they have reason to know who it is. They're going to his apartment to search. Praise the Lord. I know that it's going to be over soon. It's God who is bringing us out of this pit." Lifting Abby off the couch, he danced around the room humming and dipping her. She loved it and giggled like a schoolgirl.

Melanie and Jason heard the commotion, as did Mark. They all flocked to the den and witnessed their parents floating from side to side, singing and laughing. They dared not say anything to distract the emotion, but they were very interested in knowing what they were celebrating.

Abby caught the audience in her peripheral vision and said with a whimsical tone, "Your father and I are celebrating."

"Yes, we see that. Why?" Mark asked with a grin across his face that showed every tooth in his mouth.

"It's possible that they found the guy."

"The guy? They found him?" Melanie couldn't come up with anything else to say.

"Maybe. Some guy named Stanley Weber. We'll see. In the meantime, can I be alone to dance with my beautiful wife?"

He moved her gracefully across the carpet, holding her closely and barely allowing her feet to touch the floor. Melanie, Jason and Mark took the hint and dragged themselves away from the entertainment.

Jason repeated the last name, unsure of why it sounded familiar to him. "Weber."

"I can honestly say that was a shocker. I am glad that they are happier now, but I don't think I can stand to see that kind of display again," Mark commented and they all three laughed.

"Jason, do you know what this may mean? It may be over. It may all be over!" Her smile and eyes had a restful look on them as she squeezed Jason and Mark in a double hug.

"I want to think that it's true, but, I just have to see the proof." Jason disappointed them both with the comment, but he had no idea what proof he would receive.

"Oh, come on. Don't ruin this for me. I am finally going to sleep soundly and not wake up with my insides screaming. Can't you look at it a better way than this?"

"Mel, you know I want to but I don't want our hopes to get too high. We thought we already put the guy in prison, but it appears that we haven't. I just want to know for sure. You should, too."

"Mark, you can celebrate with me, can't you?"

"Yeah, if there's ice cream. I do agree with Jason a little. What if it's not the man, what if it's just another dead end?"

"Fine. I'll be as doubtful as the two of you. But, I still have faith that God is in total control and that the man will be found, if he hasn't been already."

They strolled into the kitchen and tore into a tub of Rocky Road.

Margaret's phone rang several times before she answered it. The machine would have picked up on the next ring, but she refused to allow herself to paralyze every time something happened. It seemed that everything had completely stopped but she stayed on alert. She knew that if she were going to help in any way, she had to play the victim to the hilt.

"Yeah. Margaret Ritchey."

"Margaret, this is Glenn Crawford. I just thought I'd call and let you know that there has been a crack in the case and the police are taking a warrant over to search someone's house. They think it's him."

"Oh, good. Can I quit playing the game now?"

"Well, just to be on the safe side, wait until there is an arrest made. Hey, wouldn't it be weird if you had to represent this person? I know, sick joke. Sorry. Well, I'll let you go. Just thought you'd be interested."

"Thanks, Glenn."

As she laid the phone down, the tension between her eyes began to give way as did the contractions in her neck. She didn't realize that she'd been wound so tightly, until the release came.

She grabbed her cup of hot tea, slid into the couch under a blanket and pulled out a book. The soft meow of her precious calico baby came pouncing on her knees. It wandered up to the book and covered it completely with its tail as it swished back and forth caressing her cheeks with its whiskers. She didn't mind the distraction. *Finally, things might be back to normal,* she thought.

"Maybe I ought to try a new line of work. You think I'd make a good prosecutor, Baby? That's fine. I know you love me anyway, don't you sugar?" Their noses touched as she nuzzled the soft smooth fur in her arms.

The conversations with her cat were the only companionship she knew and she frankly enjoyed her solitude. She was around people all day long and the last thing she wanted to come back home to was another person and twice the amount of laundry. Although, at times, it would be nicer to talk to someone who would actually talk back, share thoughts with and just cuddle up to. She let out a pitiful sigh as she said a quick prayer asking for someone to enter her life.

Not five minutes had gone by when the phone rang again. She was glad it was a cordless, since the cat was atop her like a statue. She would have hated to disturb his comfort. To her surprise, it was Jeffrey Conrad. She looked up at the ceiling, winked and mouthed, "Thank you, God."

The door was locked with a chain and deadbolt. Stan heard several footsteps lead to his apartment. He sat frozen at his desk in the closet. Knocks became louder and he could hear his neighbors coming out of their quarters questioning what the commotion could be. He made no moves to open the door. If it was going to be this easy to find him, it had to be a little difficult to get him to cooperate and open the door for his arrest.

The door hinges cracked loudly as a tall brawny man pushed his way into the stark habitat that Stan had created for himself. What seemed like thousands of people, were only three policemen. They looked around commenting on the poor lawn chair, which sat in the front room. The fact that there was no television seemed unbelievable. The fridge was bare save for a few cartons of rotten milk and a dried broken egg on the shelf. It was far less than a bachelor pad. It didn't even have a recliner or frozen dinners.

Stan sneered into the mirror as he put on the mask of Evan Garrison Jurney one last time. He pressed it close to his face but without the glue to hold it in place, it hung loosely as if skin were peeling off in sheets. He smiled and played the end over and over in his head. His bedroom door opened as men in blue uniforms came barging in flashing a warrant and a badge and several guns. The closet door was wide open as he looked at the men from behind the eyes of another man. "Gentlemen. I know what you have come for."

The men faced him with a look of horror and question. *Who is this nutcase?* they wondered. *What is with the mask?* Then with a sudden jolt, they all realized that they were looking at Evan Jurney's face. It was paralyzing.

He didn't try to hide anything. He slowly took off the mask revealing his own identity. Officer Myers looked at him closely as he asked him politely to hand over the mask, while maintaining a good grip on the gun pointed at Stan. As Myers inspected it closely, he noticed the resemblance. "This is supposed to be Evan Jurney isn't it, Mr. Weber?"

Stan just nodded and smiled. With pride, he exclaimed in a fearfully calm, slow deliberate voice, "I made it myself. I did a fine job, don't you think? It took just a short time to make the perfectly colored latex. I enjoyed wearing it as I sat in the jury box during the trial. Did you enjoy the trial? I only wish I could have had more time there. The trial was over way too quickly. It should have been easier to pin it on the lowlife in the defense seat. He wasn't worth the vinyl chair they put him in. I can't believe how that lady attorney, you know, Ms. Ritchey, was so unprepared in her defense. It's like she didn't even try to find a way to keep it going."

"Pardon me, Mr. Weber, but I believe that we need to take you down to the station. Do you understand what we're doing? I'm not sure if you understand that you have said quite a lot that a court will hold you responsible for. What I'm saying is that you have the right to remain silent, anything..." Stan interrupted and rolled his eyes. He'd heard it millions of times on television and he didn't need to use his rights. He didn't think that he had rights, even when he was a child.

"I know, but you don't seem to understand me at all. I have played the game and I lost. It's my punishment and I accept it. I know what's in store for me. It's not that I am scared. I will finally be able to get away from the fear of knowing what to say to him."

Myers was confused. "Who? Who do you want to say something to?"

"Jason. I know I should have just done it a year ago, but the fact is, I'm shy. I'm not a very stable young man but I just couldn't figure out how to approach him. You know, I only wanted to know him. I never thought I would be so angry at him. He had it all. He had her, he had a father who actually wanted him around, and I bet he didn't have to live like I did. The masks represent the pain that I have felt and the pain that others should understand." His face became hard and his eyes looked sharp and crossed. He suddenly became threatening and very aggressive. His hands reached out to Myers' gun, but before he could grab it Myers yelled. The gunshots rang loudly in Stan's ears as he fell to the floor in a heap. His blood poured out in every direction. He looked at the officers and placed his hands in his pocket. Holding out a yellow legal paper, he made a last request in a slow, broken, child-like voice.

"Please, give this to my brother. Jason will understand that when he gets my letter. Please deliver it to him and kiss my Melanie for me. Tell, him I'm sorry."

"Your brother? Jason is your brother?" Myers was stunned but no answer came from Stan's mouth.

His eyes fluttered uncontrollably as the life escaped his mouth and he lay there in his own blood pool with vacant eyes staring up into nothingness.

The shocking events didn't keep the men from doing their jobs. They rounded up all of the closet evidence and then searched the kitchen for any serrated knives they could find. Soon everything was bagged and labeled and the men filed out of the apartment.

Officer Myers opened the note and read, with a terrified, yet heartbroken look upon his face.

The uniformed men stood outside the apartment for a few minutes waiting for the body to be wheeled out, before they took off to the station.

Officer Myers took the note over to the dormitory. "No, he's not here. I assume he's with Melanie."

He drove to the Crawfords' house and was greeted at the door by Glenn, who looked at him with anxiousness.

He nodded solemnly, "It's over, Mr. Crawford. We got the guy. His name is Stan Weber. He told us everything we needed in order to convict, but a struggle ensued and he was shot three times. He asked me to make sure that Jason received this. I'll stay and make sure everything is fine."

"Jason, the officer is here for you."

"This is for you. It's from Stan Weber."

"Who? Stan Weber? I don't know any Stan Weber."

"He said he is, was your brother."

Jason felt flush and weak as he recalled scenes flashing of his mother and her older son. "That's what my mother's last name was, Weber."

Dear Jason,

I guess if you have this in your hands, I am found out. I know it wasn't easy, these past months. They've been rough on me as well. I tried so hard in the fall to find a way to introduce myself but I had no words that seemed easy to explain who I was, or why you would even want to know me. I'll just spit it out. You are my brother. I am three years older than you and you were spared the life that I had to endure. Mother couldn't keep you so seven months after you were born she took me and hid us in a different state. Marcus didn't try to find us. He wasn't my father so I was of little concern to him. He was glad that she was gone, I'm sure. I know this comes as a shock to you. You have a brainy brother. You should know, I grew up loving you. I kept this picture wherever I was. It's you and me. You were only four months old but I was so proud of you. It was hard to leave the only thing that really ever loved me back. You were unconditional.

Mother, or as I like to refer to her, the dead woman in the picture, was an addict of everything under the sun. She didn't like me. I was more than her punching bag; I was also her tension releaser. When she didn't have anything else to do, she would send me to my room and then come in to take advantage of a little boy. A little boy who learned to hate early and trade places with another identity. I became as smart as I could just to be someone else, someone who made others proud. Only teachers noticed the good in me. I found you and I came here just to see you, but I didn't know if you would love me or see worthiness in me. I saw you as the one who got out of the hurt the easy way. I saw you with your pretty little girlfriend and I saw you have friends, and family. I didn't have that. I had nothing. I built what I had and it still wasn't anything. I guess you can rest assured that you are safe. I will miss you coming in to get coffee. I will miss you and I'm sorry that you became my enemy. I only wanted to have you love me as your big brother. Please forgive me.

Stan Weber, your older brother

Jason stood in shock. He didn't know how to respond, with anger or with fear or with sadness. Every feeling flooded at the same time and he was overwhelmed with emotion. His eyes dripped water while Melanie held him closely. "Oh Jason. I'm so sorry. I'm so sorry. You had no idea, Jason. You couldn't have known."

His sobs became silent as he looked up from her shoulder and held the picture in his hand. He didn't recognize anyone in it, including himself. "Where is he?" Jason asked, not knowing what answer he was hoping for.

"He's dead. He got shot while we were trying to arrest him. It wouldn't help you to see him now. It's all over."

"Not really. It's not all over. I didn't get my answers."

"What do you want to know?"

"What? He told you? Okay Officer, why did he rape her? Why didn't he come after me? Why didn't he just forget he was even related to me? Why did he hate me? It wasn't my fault, you know."

Glenn hugged Jason, "It's not wrong to feel angry. You have the right, but remember that God got us through the bad stuff. This is the end. It's the conclusion. Let it all out now. Don't keep questioning, what you couldn't have known or changed in the first place."

Jason fell to his knees and clung to Glenn's ankles, while the rest of the family knelt beside him and covered him with their hands. His sobs were uncontrollable as he prayed aloud a humbling prayer.

His words wouldn't come out easily and he struggled to say something that could possibly bring him peace and rest in the midst of the anguish. "God, forgive the anger that I am feeling. Please give me the grace to love this man, my brother. Please Father, strengthen us now, in you."

The Crawfords held Jason closely as he wept tears of hurt that turned into tears of mercy on someone he had no remembrance of. He didn't know that at such an early age, someone could hurt so badly and seek to find happiness in any way imaginable, even at the expense of others. He wondered if Stan ever found happiness. He guessed that he didn't know what happiness would be like anyway. Jason's heart sank and he knew that God's grace had come upon him. He forgave with no regret.

Melanie held his hand tightly and they prayed together for the time to come when every hurt would be resolved to love.

Epilogue

When the small funeral for Stan Weber was over and the charges against Gabe Shaw were dropped, things began to resume as normal. Melanie still continued to see the doctor to make sure she was not infected with any diseases when the news came.

"Melanie, I have done some testing and I think you will be excited to find out that you will be able to produce children. You are fine. Everything looks fine." The doctor left the room while Melanie changed out of the smock and into her own clothes. Jason noticed her face beaming as she walked past him in the waiting room.

"You ready?" she asked.

"Yeah. What? What are you doing?"

"I can have children." She allowed her smile to cover her entire face as it glittered in her eyes and her cheeks pushed out.

"No, are you serious? Oh praise the Lord!" She laughed a giddy laugh as he lifted her off the ground in a huge bear hug. The waiting room was filled with people who stared at the couple in their moment of euphoria. The room broke out in applause.

Jason and Melanie didn't hear anything. They only saw the Hand of God working harder and harder just for them.

Once again, Christ had proven his faithfulness.

Printed in the United States
773400001B

9 781591 298403